Dreams Unleashed

Book One

The Prophecies
A Dystopian Trilogy

Linda Hawley

NOVELS BY LINDA HAWLEY

Dreams Unleashed

Guardian of Time

Wisdom Keepers

Printed in the United States of America

Second Edition

This book is a work of fiction. Names, characters, places, events, technologies, and organizations are either products of the author's imagination or are used fictitiously. Any resemblance to actual events, locales, or persons, living or dead, is entirely coincidental.

Manuscript Edited by D Kai Wilson - IndieUnbound.com

Manuscript Proofread by Jackie Jones - JJProofing.com

Cover Design by Joleene Naylor

Print Book Design by Linda Hawley – LindaHawley.com

Cover Image:

© Filograph through Dreamstime.com

Published by Nouveau Publishing

ISBN: 1466374179
ISBN-13: 978-1466374171

DEDICATION

For Paul
You are the reason I was able to publish these words.
My love is yours for eternity.

ACKNOWLEDGMENTS

I must sincerely thank Kai Wilson for her expertise and work ethic in editing this second edition of Dreams Unleashed. Kai is an extraordinary woman, and I am proud to associate with her.

My proofreader, Jackie Jones, also deserves praise for making Dreams Unleashed readable. I have never spelled well, and her eye was an absolute necessity. She too is an exceptional woman and a gifted proofreader.

To Ed, David, Johnathan, Joseph, Julia, Jackie, Jackie the Younger, Alex, Grace, Patty, Ryan, and Joey—you each are more beloved by my soul than you will ever realize.

Lastly, I must thank my husband, Paul, and my daughters, Alexandra Elinor Hawley and Grace Katheryn Hawley. You have believed in me, let me have the time I needed to write, and never complained. I could not have written The Prophecies without your selfless love and excitement for this story. You are my heart; I would be nothing without you.

NOTE TO THE READER

Since Dreams Unleashed is the first book in The Prophecies series, you'll learn a great deal in the pages to come about characters and events that will play out in the coming books. You'll be going with my heroine, Ann Torgeson, on some flashbacks all the way back to the year 1988. I suggest that you pay attention to the chapter headings, to help keep your bearings.

CHAPTER 1
WASHINGTON, D.C.

I hurried off the metro at the Union Station stop, looking around to see if anyone followed.

Okay so far, I silently encouraged myself.

After quickly negotiating the crowd, I approached the escalator. Taking the steps two by two, I tried to make my body move as smoothly as possible so that I wouldn't attract attention. I kept touching the moving handrail, trying to ground myself, though my heart was nearly beating out of my chest.

How could they have known?

After climbing halfway up the escalator, I was blocked by an elderly couple.

Move…move…move, please! I wanted to shout.

But they didn't move.

Looking up to the turn-of-the-century arched ceiling far above me, I tried to relieve my anxiety. With a jerk, the escalator reached the top and dumped me out. I moved around the couple and began to walk as fast as I could, passing through the eighteenth-century columns, walking evenly on the marble floor. The main hall was filled with people, all of them busy, seeming to move in every direction at once. I could smell the grease from the food court and felt bile rise up in my throat.

Focus on the light…focus on the light…you can make it, I coached myself.

I could see the exits under the three archways directly in front of me. Weaving through the masses, I tried to make my way to the doors. Reaching them, I passed under the centurion statues and pushed past a rush of people going the opposite direction. I collided with a man but pressed forward, still trying to get away.

After passing through the door, I looked behind me, half expecting to see pursuers. I ran across the loading and unloading lane and was nearly hit by an eager driver. Grateful to reach the brick walkway that surrounded the Christopher Columbus fountain, I stood behind it, breathing deeply. This would block me from the view of anyone in the station.

Regroup, Ann.

I had hastily gotten off the metro at Union Station, thinking that it would be easier to lose myself in the middle of D.C. than in Pentagon City, where the FBI had chased me. After meeting my contact there, we saw almost too late that we'd been shadowed. We then split up using the standard protocol.

Think quickly, I urged myself.

From behind the fountain, I carefully glanced to the entrance of the station, but my wrist was painfully grabbed from the other side by the crew-cut twenty-something I had bumped into earlier.

If he's here—that means there's more.

I whipped around and, with my free hand, shoved my Taser into his groin, delivering 2.7 million volts of resistance, while simultaneously yanking my other wrist away as hard as I could. Almost instantly, the man crumpled at my feet, and I sprinted away.

My mind raced. *Where can I go?* Panic gripped me, but I tried to think clearly. *Kelly's restaurant*, I thought. It was only a couple of blocks away, and I could call from there.

Scrambling across Columbus Circle, I ran west on Massachusetts Avenue.

It should only take me a couple of minutes. F-street…it's on F…I think. I knew Brian Kelly, the owner, and a couple of the waiters at Kelly's Irish Times from my time as a journalist in D.C. If one of them was there getting ready to open for dinner, they would let me in.

When I saw a break in traffic, I ran across Massachusetts Avenue and glanced to my left to see if anyone was pursuing me.

All clear.

After hightailing it up F-street, I finally reached the green awning marking Kelly's. I knocked on the door, slowing my breathing, and hoped there was someone there that I knew.

If I can just get inside, they'll never think to look for me here with the restaurant closed.

I knocked for about fifteen seconds, seeming like an eternity, and then saw Brian approach the door wearing a stained white cook's apron.

"You know we're not open for another hour or…Ann, lass. It's been a while now, hasn't it? Come on in then," he said eagerly, opening the door.

I stepped in and turned once more to see if I was followed. It looked safe.

Brian closed the door and reached down to hug me with his stocky frame. I could feel his bristly beard on my neck as he briefly squeezed me. He put his pudgy hands on both of my shoulders and peered down to me with his dark eyes.

"To what do I owe this pleasure?" he asked. His deep, smooth voice held a note of concern.

"I'm working on something that's gotten a little tricky. Do you think I could use your bathroom and make a call?" I asked.

"Of course. You take all the time you need," he said.

"Thank you," I said gratefully.

"If you need anything, you come get me," he said, patting my shoulder, then looking out the window before he locked the front door and walked back toward the kitchen.

I had known Brian for many years. While I was a reporter, he occasionally gave me insider tips on stories I was working on. I knew I could rely on his discretion. After making my way to the back of the restaurant, I pulled open the green wooden door of the women's bathroom. The door looked like it had been painted one too many times.

Inside, every available space of the light brown bathroom walls bore plaques bearing Irish platitudes. I set my messenger bag in one of the two vintage sinks and plugged my used Taser into an outlet near the floor. Then I pulled my second Taser from the bag and put it in my coat pocket.

Standing there at the sink, looking at my reflection in the mirror, I prepared myself to make the call. I needed help.

I dialed and waited as the cell phone rang three times. "Hi…leave me a—"

Crap—Bob's voicemail.

I tried to consider my options. I could call the clandestine switchboard, but they might already have me flagged. That wouldn't work.

I'm a fugitive now. They're hunting me. They think of me as a weapon. Plus, I just Tasered crew-cut boy. I'm gonna have to go underground now, I thought grimly.

Reaching into the bag, I pulled out the Ziploc bag containing the last secure cell phone I had. I quickly assembled it, then pressed the timer of my watch.

I called the local phone number I had memorized.

"B40 for extraction, code red," I said urgently upon hearing the beep.

I hung up and watched my timer. I had four minutes before I had to destroy the phone. I looked up and noticed one of the wall plaques, "May the bearer of the news be safe."

No kidding, I thought ironically.

Thirty seconds later, the call came.

"Yes," I answered.

"Code?" he asked.

"Cherry blossoms," I replied, using the memorized code.

"D.C.," he confirmed. "We've got your location. Seven minutes—we're en route—back alley. Injuries?"

"No."

"Stay safe," he said, crisp but cautious.

Hanging up, I looked at my watch to see how long the phone had been traceable.

Three minutes—maybe they didn't locate me.

After pulling the phone apart, I stomped on it and threw all the pieces in the sink, turning on the faucet. The soft sound of the running water would have been calming in any other situation.

I restarted my stopwatch. *They'll be here in seven minutes.* Grabbing the pieces of the cell phone from the sink, I tossed them back into the Ziploc and threw the bag in the empty trashcan, covering it with some clean paper towels.

I have to stay here...they won't be able to find me if I leave, since that was my last safe phone.

Three minutes.

Pounding on the front door of the restaurant sent a buzz of adrenaline through me. *They found me.*

I quickly grabbed the recharging Taser from the wall and tossed it into my messenger bag, which I draped across my body, freeing my hands. Slowly opening the bathroom door, I slipped into the dark back hall. I could hear Brian's deep, full voice from the next room.

"Can I help you?" he asked coldly.

"FBI," said a male voice. "We're looking for a woman who's in this area, about 5'9", Caucasian, midforties. Seen her?"

Brian didn't hesitate. "We're closed; haven't opened for dinner yet."

Silently thanking Brian, I moved down the narrow hall toward the battered, brown service door. Touching the button for light on my watch, I checked the time. Less than two minutes. I tried not to panic, though adrenaline was tingling through me in rushing bolts.

The conversation between them was so distant that I couldn't hear it. Preparing myself to open the door, I pulled the second Taser from my pocket, looped the strap around my wrist, and instinctively pushed the button to turn it on. If anyone tried to grab it from me, the loop would pull out the arming pin, disabling it.

Turning the dented brass knob, I pushed open the back door slightly, peering out into the alley. My eyes fell upon an overflowing dumpster for a brief second, and then the door was yanked open from the outside. I turned to run, but a crew-cut clone grabbed me by the hair. I twisted around and was able to jam the Taser into his exposed armpit, and he fell to the ground, convulsing with a heavy thud. As my hair was released, the SUV rounded the corner of the alley, and I ran for it, hoping I was running toward friends.

CHAPTER 2

BELLINGHAM, WASHINGTON THE YEAR 2015

I sat up in bed, drenched in sweat.

"Oh man, that was a bad one," I said out loud to no one. The details of my dream lingered with me as though they were real. I wiped the sweat from my face with my sheet. My heart was doing double time as the adrenaline still coursed through my body.

What was that about?

My mind raced to try to make sense of the disturbing dream. I'd had numerous others like it; chase dreams seemed to be the specialty of my sleeping mind lately.

I needed to get ready for work. AlterHydro was waiting.

Driving to work, the dream marinated in my mind.

I'd been working at my desk for about an hour when my phone rang. After one ring, I answered.

"Hi, Bennett. What can I do for you?" I said, voice imitating an enthusiastic employee.

I already knew his reason for calling, and I nodded to no one in particular as I tried to convince him that everything was on track for the first draft of the new turbine manual. It seemed to be his pet project, and I tried to hide the exasperation in my voice, steeling myself for his generous critique.

"No problem, Bennett. I can be there in ten minutes. Will that work for you?" I asked with a cheerfulness that made my jaw ache.

You would think that after three years of working for him, he'd have some degree of faith in my ability to write a good technical manual.

"What a control freak," I muttered angrily, then looked around to see if my co-workers had heard me.

I should have known that he'd be a nightmare when I interviewed for this job.

It was the fourth interview—this time with Bennett's younger brother—that nearly made me ditch the idea of working at AlterHydro.

"Ann Torgeson," he said, shaking my hand. "I'm Brock Pressentin. Have a seat," he said with authority. He sat down, leaned back in his chair, put his feet on the long conference-room table, and smugly started with, "So, Ann, tell me about yourself."

I blinked in surprise. This was his interview ritual, I knew, but his casual cockiness bothered me. I was a professional technical writer and was certainly a good hire for any Fortune 100 company; I expected to be treated with respect by potential employers. The only reason I wanted to work for AlterHydro, which was *not* a Fortune 100 company, was because of their unique innovation in alternative energy. To say that I was annoyed by Brock's freshman interview style was an understatement.

As I prepared to answer him, Bennett barged into the room, taking a seat next to his little brother while pushing his sibling's feet off the table.

"Hi, Ann. Hi, Brock," he quickly offered with a smile.

Along with my greeting, I forced a pleasant smile.

Silence seethed from baby brother as he stared at his sibling.

"My last meeting finished early, so I thought I'd sit in on your interview," Bennett announced to me. It was an obvious preemptive strike to Brock's rejection of his unexpected presence.

"Like I was saying, why don't you tell me about yourself?" Brock continued, turning to me, this time with a louder voice, his eyebrows tensed.

Looking from brother to brother, I suddenly realized that this family dysfunction was something I didn't want to be a part of. Just as I was speed formulating my "I don't think we're a good fit" speech, I received a friendly wink and smile from Bennett.

It took me only a moment to realize that I was a small piece in a family game of "appease the younger brother so I can hire you."

Okay, I'll bite. I enjoyed banter and was curious to see how the dynamic between the two brothers played out. I plowed ahead.

"As I'm sure you've seen from my résumé, I have significant experience as a technical writer with the government. I'm bound by confidentiality not to discuss those projects specifically, but I can tell you that I wrote about cutting-edge technologies, complicated in both design and scope. Writing for Black Projects was challenging because I had to understand the hardware and software well enough to write for both technical and non-technical readers. Before that, I—"

"How can you expect me to assess whether you're qualified for this position unless you tell me what you actually worked on?" Brock interrupted, smugness dripping from his voice.

"That's a good question," I answered patiently. "I'm sure you'll agree, though, that if I were to share that information with you, I would not only be breaking confidentiality with my previous employer, but I would also be betraying our country's secrets. My ability to keep confidences will be an asset to you, if I'm hired by AlterHydro."

Brock Pressentin opened his mouth to say something but apparently couldn't think of a rebuttal.

Game, set, match.

Bennett saw that his brother had been aced in our verbal tennis game and seized the interview.

"Ann, tell us what you can bring to AlterHydro from your experience with the government and as a journalist," Bennett instructed.

Elder brother's redirection of the interview, and my witness to his intuition in doing so, influenced me to stay the course and complete the interview process. As long as I worked directly for Bennett, and not Brock, I could find satisfaction in writing about AlterHydro's energy solutions.

Their Bellingham location north of the Puget Sound, where the Strait of Georgia met the Strait of Juan de Fuca, was the Everest of tidal action, with energy perpetually created. Channels and headlands further accelerated the energy. Because tidal turbines were anchored on the seabed far beneath the ocean's surface, they were neither seen nor heard by man, which was a significant asset. AlterHydro was the first company in the Pacific Northwest to capture this supercharged energy. I was willing to move from the East Coast to the West to be a part of it. The timing was good, too. I was looking forward to the move, which would bring me back to where my husband, Armond, was buried.

During that first interview with Bennett, his passion for the technology was palpable—and contagious.

"Do you realize," he asked me with excitement during the first interview, "that if less than 0.1 percent of ocean energy could be turned into electricity, no one on the earth would need fossil fuel?"

I was interested in that. I wanted to know that my work would mean something.

When I was hired by AlterHydro, the entire company was a ball of energy. It held some of the most valuable patents in the world. It was my job to write the technical manuals for the turbine. I was also responsible for writing the content for sales materials on the benefits of tidal power. With fossil fuels continuing to climb and gasoline selling for over eight dollars per gallon, it wasn't difficult to get caught up in the high morale present at the company.

Working for Bennett proved to be challenging, however. He was, as in the interview when I first met him, charming, personable, passionate, and intuitive. But he was also arrogant, and he frequently flaunted his Mensa-level intelligence to overpower others. His being a control freak was only icing on the cake.

I had to mentally prepare myself to meet with him this morning.

Come on, you'd better go see him.

I took a long drink of my Mountain Dew to force sugar-induced over-enthusiasm, then stood from my desk, scooping up the latest version of the technical manual.

"Lulu, stay," I gently commanded my dog after she rose to follow me. "You wouldn't want to go with me anyway, girl."

One of the fringe benefits of working at AlterHydro was that we could bring our dogs to work. Lulu was a Brittany Spaniel I had bought as a puppy from a private breeder I'd met in Washington three years before. Easily trained as a puppy, she now knew more than twenty commands. Lulu came to work with me every day, watching and smelling the goings-on with curiosity.

Pausing at my desk, I looked at the other basement dwellers of the 1910, the name we called our century-old building. I loved the old brick building; it was where the town's first newspaper had started. We shared common journalistic roots, and even though the 1910 had been renovated many years before, the old smells of ink and paper seemed to linger like its own earthy perfume.

My stream of consciousness shifted subtly from the smell of the 1910 to the smell of Bennett's Calvin Klein cologne.

Ugh.

One of my lesser-known, more unfortunate abilities was my acute sense of smell. I couldn't explain it, really, but it was true; if it was there, I could smell it. My smelling abilities were more of a curse than a blessing; there are some things that no human should ever have to smell. It wasn't just the smells themselves that overpowered me. I also, for some inexplicable reason, had an overdeveloped smell memory.

From a smell, I could remember the situation I was in when I first smelled it, which was occasionally useful, but mostly annoying. It was similar to a photographic memory, but sensory. Some smells triggered intense flashbacks to memories I'd worked to forget. But there was no help for it; it was sensory déjà vu.

When I was in my freshman year of college, I briefly dated a guy whose putrid breath could not be disguised by his frequent and liberal use of Calvin Klein cologne. Though Bennett's breath was significantly better than that of the guy I'd dated in college, his cologne choice still brought on halitosis flashbacks.

There was no need to take the vintage elevator to meet with Bennett; it would take three minutes and thirty-three seconds for the elevator to arrive in the basement. I had timed it one day while waiting. It was as though the elevator itself was reluctant to enter the dark abyss. I could walk up the stairs to Bennett's office faster.

At least I'll burn a few calories while I'm at it.

I took the stairs two at a time. I'd been a runner all my life, and because of the number of calories expended through long-distance running, I ate what I wanted when I wanted but still remained fit and toned. I was vainly proud of my round behind, even though most long-distance runners had no booty to speak of. Men always told me that my spirit was young, but I think they may have been looking at my backside.

I took in a deep breath. *Only two flights to go.*

At forty-four years old, I'd come into my own in so many ways. I had my daughter, Elinor, who was now away at her first year of college. I was technically an empty nester, which felt odd, considering that I still felt so young.

As I arrived on the top floor, where Bennett's Calvin Klein cologne beckoned me, I braced myself for the nasty déjà vu to come. My too-frequent silent self-talk began as I started my death-row trek down the wide art-lined hall to the huge corner office. I had been there many times, in its urban luxury, with sparse furnishings that drew the eye toward the sea through the floor-to-ceiling windows that faced Bellingham Bay. Bennett was a sailor and loved the water. When he first gave me a tour of his office, he told me that he had chosen it for the corner view of the bay to help him think.

I knocked once on his open door, and he looked up and replied with a smile, "Come on in, Ann."

"Hi, Bennett," I warmly offered, handing over the manual while attempting to hold my breath and smile at the same time, amid the sea of Calvin Klein.

"Hey, Ann. Thanks for bringing this up. I really wanted to look it over before you got too far down the path. I really should have seen it sooner. I didn't realize that you were already writing this section," Bennett responded with annoyance.

His concern was unwarranted. It seemed like he should have bigger concerns as the company's president, and I didn't understand why he insisted on keeping such a close eye on the progress of the technical manual. I tried to refrain from frowning; it wasn't as though he was grooming me for management. There was no such thing as upward mobility at AlterHydro.

"I thought I'd get a head start," I answered. "I know it's your keystone project this quarter." My smile was forced, and I hoped he wouldn't notice. "I can see you want to look through it, so why don't I just pop back later to pick it up?" I turned to go, but he stopped me before I could reach the door.

"Oh no, I won't need it for very long," he interrupted. "Hang tight for a few minutes—have a seat," he said, gesturing to the chair.

Oh please, not again. I reluctantly sat on the very edge of the seat across from the huge oak desk. *The last time this happened, I was here for forty-five minutes while he read the manual…sitting here with the memory of putrid-breath hijacking my mind.*

Just as I was resigning myself to a morning of torture, Bennett closed the cover of the manual and said, "You know, Ann, I think I'd like to spend a bit more time reading this. I'll have my assistant send it back to you later, okay?"

I perked up from my perch, genuinely smiled, and replied, "Sure. No problem. Glad to help."

"Ann," Bennett called out as I was escaping through the door.

"Yes?" I replied, turning back towards him.

"You look nice today. That color sets off the light blue in your eyes."

"Thanks. Enjoy that manual." I smiled as I left his office.

I'm a sucker for a compliment, dang it. If he'd lay off the Calvin Klein, I might be able to like him.

I strode down the hall toward the stairs, eager to find fresh air.

It wasn't until I was a few steps away that the thought dawned on me. *Is he hitting on me again?* I hoped not.

Last year when we were on a business trip together in San Francisco, Bennett got hammered on Tequila shots after our dinner and started flirting openly with me. Chalking it up to the numerous drinks he'd had, I had let the flirtations slide. His 5'6" height combined with his skinny one hundred twenty pounds didn't ignite anything in me. We were simply not compatible physically. Even with his piercing ocean-blue eyes, I couldn't be tempted.

I was skilled at deflecting flirtations by executives, having refined my technique during my years as a reporter. No woman could be a successful journalist without becoming an expert in the art of the sexual brush-off. I did have a gift for extracting information from drunken sources, though, without offending my target's sensitive ego or getting myself in sticky situations.

During the same evening of drunkenness, Bennett unloaded on me the full details about how he wanted to leave his family's business and start out on his own. He had great dreams of developing his own innovative new technology so that he could break free of the family.

I used my refined deflecting maneuver in dealing with flirtatious Tequila-Bennett, even when he tried to cop a feel of my bootie that night.

Did he even remember that? Well, I made it through another encounter, I thought, cruising toward the stairwell.

I opened the door and sucked in a deep breath of stairwell air, nearly running into the vice president of sales, Blake Benz.

"Hi, Blake," I offered with an enthusiastic smile.

He burst out laughing. "You didn't have to endure the Calvin Klein again, did you, Annie?"

Ever since I had my job interview with Blake, the only non-family member of the executive staff, I had good rapport with him. He was attractive, in his midthirties, and had a head of short, thick, dark brown hair that he styled with gel. His hazel eyes twinkled when he smiled, and his face was covered with freckles. He was my height, with a bulky athletic body; he knew he was attractive but didn't flaunt it. He never wore a tie in the office, instead opting for Izod golf shirts.

Blake was the office sports junkie; he ran the fantasy football league and coached his son's baseball team. He had an easy laugh with a dry sense of humor. Blake was professional when I interviewed for the job and gave me the thumbs up for hire. He was always politically correct and seemed to have full control of his emotions and what he shared with others, but he wasn't reserved. In a nutshell, Blake was everything that I wasn't. He was admired by both the family executives and his sales team. Blake was the only one in the company to call me Annie, a name he'd adopted for me suddenly one day and had called me ever since.

"Ooh, that Calvin Klein was screamin' today," I responded sarcastically.

He laughed.

"Now what would life be, Annie, if you didn't have that kind of excitement?"

"Hmmm." I smiled, pretending to seriously consider his question. "Refreshing?"

"So, how are things with the basement exiles?" teased Blake.

"What do ya mean? Those are my people."

Chuckling sincerely, he replied, "I gotta run, Annie. Bennett asked for these sales estimates."

"Oh, okay."

"Hey, rock on," he added, his classic end for stairwell chitchat.

Lulu greeted me when I arrived downstairs again. "Hi, girl," I said, patting her on the head. She sniffed me. "I know, you smell it too, don't you?" I asked, petting her attentively.

Back at my desk, breathing the comforting musty basement air, I dove into my chocolate stash that I kept in the bottom left drawer of my desk. I had earned a treat. After a few pieces of my milk-chocolate-covered raspberry decadence, I leaned back in my chair and looked around at the 1910 basement exiles. There were only two of them.

Paul, a computer geek, was the genius behind all the company's software technology. He was a beautiful man, tall, with a lanky body, short blond hair, and intense brown eyes. I was sure that Paul had a six-pack underneath his shirt, and from time to time I fantasized boldly walking over to him and simply cutting his shirt off with my scissors to verify the fact. He had an easy smile and laugh and a great sense of weird humor. His wealthy parents had sent him to Harvard when he was only sixteen. It was commonly known at AlterHydro that the Pressentins thought that Paul walked on water. He was about as close as you got to being *in the family*.

Paul was well kept. He also had a crush on me since the day I arrived at AlterHydro. He'd never really made the effort to pursue me, but I knew of his attraction by his attentiveness and the way he always smiled at me when making eye contact. Paul was the whole package, and from time to time I needed to remind myself to forget that. There were rules against employees dating, and the last thing I wanted to do was get fired because I couldn't keep my hands to myself.

Edwin, the other basement exile, was a mechanical engineer who designed the tidal turbines and ensured that the Chinese-manufactured products were free of engineering defects. He was five foot nine, handsome, with jet-black hair and kind, dark eyes. It seemed that every week Edwin was testing some new material in the basement. He also had a regular habit of blowing up food in the microwave. Edwin was Chinese and one of the most book-smart men I had ever known. He worked hard to fit into American culture, but it seemed to be impossible for him. He spoke perfect English, but no slang ever slipped through his lips nor did he ever use contractions in speech, so he always sounded so formal. Edwin was socially awkward, lived in his head, and was always concerned about American propriety. I wanted to tell him that Americans in 2015 no longer had any real propriety, but I didn't want to break his heart. When Edwin didn't know something, he kept his mouth shut, unlike most Americans.

Both Paul and Edwin were in the basement for two simple reasons: they needed a good deal of space for their equipment, and their work was interconnected, with Paul writing software to run Edwin's designs. I was likely there because of the proximity to them, for they supplied much of the subject matter that I wrote about. We weren't truly *exiles*, but being in the musty basement qualified us.

After I got over the initial shock of my basement home, I was willing to find the bright side to my subterranean refuge. It was a huge space, so I chose wherever I wanted my desk to go, and even got to pick from the furniture dogpile left by ex-employees. After the first week, however, I moved my desk a second time, putting distance between Edwin's burnt microwave scents and myself. It didn't help much, though. This was one example of the downside of my smelling acuity. In time I was able to get Bennett's approval for an air filtration unit for the basement.

Getting the filtration unit was no small feat, though, given that the corporate office manager, Vicki, would balk at ordering a simple high-quality pair of scissors. She would buy the cheapest of everything because she received a quarterly bonus tied to how much she saved of her supply budget. After two pairs of scissors resembling government-issued 1950s-era models fell apart, I marched upstairs to demand that the 350-pound, polyester-covered, fifty-year-old virgin order me a decent pair of scissors. You would've thought that I'd asked the woman to donate a kidney. Vicki fought me outright, refusing to buy the scissors. Finally in complete frustration, I sent Bennett an email:

Hello Bennett:

Please authorize Vicki to order me a sharp pair of high-quality scissors. The cost is $15.99. The model is shown below.

Thank you, Ann

Bennett replied directly to the micro-manager, copying me, with a one-word email:

Approved

Bennett had been down that road with Vicki many times. It was common knowledge that he didn't think much of her; she was hired by Bennett's grandfather in his first business thirty years previously—Vicki was a Pressentin family lifer.

About two weeks after I got my high-quality scissors, they disappeared. I looked for them everywhere, and then it occurred to me that the old maid had probably stolen them, just to prove that she was the one with the power. To check my theory and to validate that paranoia wasn't actually taking root in my brain, I privately asked Paul to check the digital security log to see if she had been there the night my scissors disappeared. Sure enough, the thief came back into the building at nine that night and left fifteen minutes later. Paul said those types of events had been happening for years at AlterHydro.

I bought my own scissors and put my name on them with permanent marker.

Sometimes this place is an alternate reality, I thought, reflecting on the scissor-heist.

"It's time I go work out," I suddenly announced to no one.

Lulu stood. She knew what that meant.

As I picked up the workout bag beside my desk, I excitedly said, "Come on, Lulu." That got her bottom wagging. Brittany dogs have only a tail stub, so bottom wagging was all she could do. Her floor-polishing wobble always made me smile.

As she and I crossed the basement heading for the stairs, I smiled at Paul as he looked up from the web server he was working on, and he returned the smile.

Mmm good.

After walking up the steps and into the second-floor gym, I took my workout clothes to a dressing stall, pulled the curtain, and quickly changed. Lulu waited for me on the other side of the curtain; she knew the routine. I never was comfortable bearing it all in a gym locker room, especially after watching the movie *Carrie* one Halloween on TV when I was a kid. That movie scared the crap out of me.

Once dressed, we went into the adjacent gym and I set up Lulu on her own treadmill to the right of mine. This always elicited surprised remarks from the other employees. Then I got on my treadmill next to Lulu and started to jog. I had always used running as a therapy to work through issues.

I've gotta find a way not to let Bennett get to me. I should focus on his good qualities and stop being so annoyed that he's a control freak. Why does it matter anyway? If he were just a manager instead of an executive, you wouldn't be annoyed by his constant manual reviews, right? Right. Let it go.

In the middle of my self-therapy, Paul got on the empty treadmill on the other side of me. He was wearing running shorts that should have been outlawed after 1982. They were made of thin polyester, had a slit up the side showing the built-in underwear, and ended just below his groin.

Paul and I pleasantly chatted about work while we ran together, and the more I sweated, the less I thought about his shorts and his palatable Norwegian bloodline. I really did like Paul, and I enjoyed our physical chemistry. I was mindful and cautious of it, careful not to cross the co-worker line.

"Lulu might be running a faster mile than I am," Paul joked breathlessly.

"No, she's only at level two on the NordicTrack. It just seems faster because she's small," I joked.

Paul laughed.

We often worked out next to one another at lunch, although we never had spoken of doing so. He'd watched Lulu and I run together since I'd been at AlterHydro.

"Whenever I come in, and you're putting Lulu on the treadmill without a leash, I always watch people's expressions. At first," he said, "they look shocked. Then, when she doesn't fall off, they're really impressed," he commented with a smile, still breathless.

"She's a very cool dog," I confirmed.

"Yes, she is. Just like her mommy," he flirted.

I laughed.

After forty minutes, both Lulu and I were tired. Paul had given up before then, admitting defeat.

After my Carrie-free private shower, I headed outside with Lulu for a short walk. We then went back to my office to eat the organic salad that I had brought from home. I gave Lulu a fresh bowl of water and her lunch.

Since my job was a serious one, full of technical specifications and deadlines in addition to the stress of working for Bennett, I spent time every afternoon considering what my next vacation would be. It was my way of taking a mental break for a few minutes each afternoon.

As I dug into my salad, I thought about China. How could a country that had lagged behind the pre-industrial revolution for so long have taken over the entire American manufacturing world? I wanted to go there and experience the energy of a country that could achieve that.

CHAPTER 3
BELLINGHAM, WASHINGTON
THE YEAR 2015

Leaving the 1910, I crossed the parking lot to my sleek BYD H12 convertible. It was black with a slim silver swish around each fender. I was having a love affair with this all-electric car.

My respect for the genius CEO Wang Chuanfu influenced my decision to buy a BYD model. Chuanfu believed that a near-perfect electric car was possible, and he had been working to that end, pursuing new battery technology. He not only developed the longest-lasting and most powerful car battery, but he then developed a system to neutralize the battery without destroying it, in case it began overheating. Chuanfu was the first automotive executive to inspire me.

After my research and subsequent test drive of several BYD models, I was sold on the sleek four-door convertible the moment I sat in the plush, red leather seats. The seats reminded me of the 1960 MGA 1600 Mk I roadster that Elvis Presley drove in the movie *Blue Hawaii.* I saw the movie on television when I was twelve, and the seats were forevermore imprinted in my memory. With gas prices in the eight-dollar range now and up to twice as much outside the USA, going electric was a viable alternative to the severe prices.

As I let thoughts of work slip from my mind, I felt a small thrill as I pushed the button that would let the top down and give me a clear view of the day's precipitation-free sky. It didn't really matter that it wasn't exactly convertible weather; when I drove the BYD with the top down, the stresses of work and life in general faded away, and I felt free and relaxed.

It was finally spring; the rain had let up its punishing course from the extended winter. When I had moved from the Washington, D.C. metropolitan area to Bellingham to take the job with AlterHydro, I was captivated by all the evergreen trees and the close proximity to the Puget Sound. I had grown up in Bellingham, and it felt good to return.

After moving back in the late summer of 2012, I expected more rain, but it was August, and I guessed it had to take a break sometime. It wasn't until October that the skies themselves opened up and poured down precipitation, and it didn't stop for a solid seven months. It didn't always pour soaking rain in Bellingham; sometimes it just drizzled all...day...long. I'd arrived in Bellingham with my umbrella in hand, but three weeks into the rainy season, I trashed my umbrella and instead picked up a hooded North Face soft-shell jacket with its SecondSkin lining for warmth. I called it my *Bellslicker*, my Bellingham version of a New England rain slicker. I either wore it or kept it by my side all the time.

On the way home from work, I felt like making a pasta salad, so I stopped at the Organic Cooperative to pick up the ingredients and check out through my friend Summer's line. She and I had hit it off immediately when we first met, and we shared some lively conversations. Today it was about Pelamis and the upcoming council meeting.

She was a petite woman, about 5'2", with dyed black hair and bright-pink highlights. Her beautifully sculpted face had blazing green eyes, pale skin, and a substantial Grecian nose. She was a waif of a woman, but she was naturally quite busty. Summer was passionate about alternative energy.

"How're you doin', Ann?"

"I'm great. How are you?"

"I'm good. Did you see the latest news in Scotland with their new Sea Snake?" Summer asked with passion.

The Sea Snake was an alternative energy device that translated the waves of the sea into electricity. Developed by the Scottish company Pelamis, Sea Snake technology took off in 2011. Summer always talked about the Sea Snake; it was her go-to topic of conversation. She told me all about the current Sea Snake trials.

"The Scotts need a break after all; they're paying almost twice as much for gas as we are," I replied.

"I agree. It looks like AlterHydro and Pelamis could have a marriage in your future," Summer baited.

"No way would Bennett ever go for that," I whispered.

Summer laughed. She had grown up with Bennett in Bellingham and knew of his pride.

"Are you going to the next city council meeting?" she asked.

"I'll be there with bells on. I know that a portion of the gasoline tax is supposed to be spent on the city's social programs, but the truth is that the tax is just plugging the budget gap. We get taxed, which causes us stress, and then we need the social programs to help us with the stress. How bizarre is that?" I said, with a sardonic smile.

"You really should bring that up in the response portion of the council meeting," Summer prodded.

"The last time I made a comment in the council meeting, everyone turned and looked at me in unison, like they were clones. All those eyes," I mock shuddered.

Summer giggled with eyes wide and sparkling.

"I don't want that kind of attention, and I certainly didn't like the feeling. I think that someone with real courage needs to bring it up—like you."

"Me? No way. But I understand how you feel," she responded.

"We both complain, but then we don't want to stand up to the council."

"I know. We should be ashamed of ourselves." She winked.

"Whenever people start talking about shame, that's when I exit stage left," I commented, bagging my groceries in my cloth bag.

"Bye, hon," Summer offered with a wave of her hand.

Driving up to my house, I admired how the tulips, which lined my driveway, had come into bloom. After three years, the bulbs had finally matured into big Pacific Northwest-sized tulips.

Who would've ever known that Washington would be one of the best places in America to grow tulips?

I loved that tulips were full of vibrancy and classic shape, and for a few short weeks, they were full of living perfection. After planting nearly a hundred of them when I first moved to Bellingham, I hoped that an explosion of color each spring would ease my culture shock from my coast-to-coast move.

As I left my BYD in the driveway, I looked up at my house and was grateful that this home, with its Craftsman style, had nurtured me in this new place. I loved that it was built with classic architecture, along with the new generation of SmartWired home computer technology. I felt that my home was my friend, an ally and a protector.

As Lulu and I left the car and walked up the steps, the front door unlocked and opened automatically, using face recognition technology installed near the front door. Lulu ran in the door to drink water from her pet fountain, then to play with her toys.

She loves our home as much as I do, I thought.

As I moved through the door and into the open foyer, the front door automatically closed behind me. The lights turned on as I entered each zone. In the kitchen, I unloaded everything from the Co-Op onto the counter.

"Hello, Sinéad. New age mix," I said, addressing my SmartWired home computer.

I decided to call the home's computer Sinéad, in honor of Sinéad O'Connor. I was nineteen years old when the Irish musician's biggest CD, *I Do Not Want What I Haven't Got*, was released, and after attending her concert, I was hooked by the power and passion of the petite artist. Of course, Sinéad's independent personality also appealed to me. Whenever I felt powerless, I would play O'Connor's music to rejuvenate my spirit and remind me that I had purpose.

Naming my SmartWired home Sinéad, in the spirit of rebellion and independence, seemed right to me. SmartWired technology did have an ugly reality: it allowed the U.S. Government to track its citizens. In 2015, being tracked by anyone in the government never turned out well for the individual. So the day that I closed on my house, and before moving in a week later, I had some help from an *alternative repairman* from the underground.

CHAPTER 4
SHANGHAI, CHINA
THE YEAR 2015

I landed at Shanghai Pudong International Airport at one thirty-five p.m. on Tuesday for my meeting with the turbine manufacturer.

"Twenty-three hours in a coach seat. What could be more awful?" I muttered.

Only three hours into the flight, while I was attempting to sleep, a seemingly feeble old woman from a few rows ahead sauntered toward me and snatched the airline's mini-pillow from beneath my head.

Before I could protest the loss, the old woman leaned into my face and slurred the raspy whisky words, "I need this more than you do."

Repulsed by her pungent elder spittle, I sarcastically whispered, "Now isn't this terrific," and wiped my moist face as the drunken magician returned to her seat.

I was fuming and considered alerting a flight attendant, but then I remembered that an air marshal was likely on board and would probably enjoy restraining me. I could see him saying, "Go ahead, make my day." These days it was a very bad idea to make a big deal of anything while a mile high. So I sucked it up, swallowed my anger, and found it impossible to sleep during the next twenty hours of the transatlantic flight. Back and forth I slid and slouched my tall frame in the seat, trying to find a sleeping position that accommodated the fact that the passenger in front of me had his seat fully reclined in my lap.

When my forward companion began to snore so loudly that he nearly drowned out the sound of the jet engine, I admitted defeat, escaping into Dan Brown's latest thriller. After a few chapters, I realized that his plot was more intense than my flight.

Leaving the plane behind, I made it through customs along with my luggage without any serious problems, which was a surprising relief. I always expected to be held up at length when entering a foreign country and loathed the concentration and necessary seriousness of being interviewed for entry. Clearing through the other side of customs, I entered a crush of people from every nationality, and a collage of smells fermenting in the compact space pounced. With a nose as capable as a coonhound's, I suffered in the human holding tank while anxiously looking for the sign that would bear my name. Thank goodness I could see over the throng of bodies.

"There he is," I blurted out loudly to no one when recognizing the sign meant for me.

As I pushed through the crowd, I waved at him.

Making eye contact with me, the man holding the sign quickly nodded. Meeting me, he took my two bags and guided me to the side of the crowd. I was in awe at his skilled maneuvering.

"Good afternoon. Miss Torgeson, I presume?"

"Yes," I exhaled.

"I am Chow Lai," he said, presenting me with his business card while bowing slightly.

He spoke perfect English. *He must have gone to school in America.*

"Good afternoon, Mr. Lai. Thank you for meeting me," I replied with my practiced bow, feeling rescued by my young Chinese crowd-warrior.

He was taller than I expected, and bulkier too. Chow had kind eyes and black hair, and he stood eye to eye with me.

"I hope that your journey was pleasant, Miss Torgeson."

"Let's just say I'm happy to be here," I replied with a forced smile, unable to lie about my distressing flight, fatigue, and wrinkled clothes.

"It is never an easy journey from America," he replied directly. "If you are ready, would you like to go to the car, Miss Torgeson?"

"Yes, please. I can follow you, Mr. Lai."

When we reached the car in the airport's loading zone, the man who had been sitting in the driver's seat exited upon seeing Chow and obediently waited on the curb as a companion to my luggage. Chow held the car door for me, closed it when I was settled, and then carefully loaded my luggage into the trunk. He then handed the man some money, and the nameless placeholder walked away.

I've gotta thank Edwin for helping me find this guide, I reminded myself.

Chow took his position in the driver's seat. "Miss Torgeson, we will be driving for approximately one hour to arrive at your hotel. Please tell me if there is anything I can do to make your ride more comfortable."

"Thank you, Mr. Lai."

I asked Chow to explain the sights of Shanghai's futuristic concrete jungle. As I relaxed in the back seat, brushing through my hair, I passively took in this new, foreign world. First we drove through a section of the city that was modern China, where skyscrapers and other buildings resembled the Western world in so many ways. We entered the Bund area, which ran along the bank of the Huangpu River, north of the old walled city of Shanghai. Along the golden mile of the Bund were historic buildings built in the Romanesque, Gothic, Baroque, Neoclassical, and Art Deco architectural styles.

Before I knew it, we had arrived at the Bund Garden Hotel with a gentle stop at 200 Hankou Road. I took a deep breath as I looked out my open window. It looked as though we'd turned the clock back a century. Before me, I beheld well-manicured, beautiful gardens with sweet, spicy smells surrounding the front of the vintage hotel.

I chose this Shanghai hotel because I liked its history and symbolism.

It was built eighty-five years before, during China's communist-free Republican Era, when Shanghai was the largest cosmopolitan city in the world. It was 1930, the birth of Swing, and the sounds of Duke Ellington penetrated the Shanghai air. Yang Li was one of the progressive Chinese elite that helped modernize Shanghai into the Paris of the East. He built the Bund Hotel in honor of Song Yue, the woman he loved when he was a young man. Tragically, Yang Li was not allowed to marry Song Yue, who was a common peasant. In defiance of his elders, Yang Li saw her in secret, courting her for nine months before they were discovered.

Song Yue was found one morning, naked on the bank of the Huangpu River, having been decapitated while still alive, and in place of her head lay one perfect, long-stemmed red rose. It was a brutal but symbolic message meant for Yang Li from her killer: to defy one's elders and stray outside your class had deadly consequences. The murderer was never identified. When Yang Li was able, he built the hotel as a memorial to his lost love. He designed the hotel with only nine guest rooms, in honor of the nine months of courtship with Song Yue. Staying at the Bund Hotel was my tribute to the purity of love.

As Chow opened the car door to release me, I glided through the magnificent neo-Gothic entry, beckoned by its history. Slowly I made my way through the lobby, gazing in awe at the majestic arched window recesses and the magnificent sculpted wooden staircase in the center of the foyer.

It's peaceful. I can rest here.

I watched Chow communicate with the front-desk clerk, speaking in a Wu Chinese dialect.

He's handsome, I thought, observing Chow.

He crossed the lobby and then led me up the grand staircase. I slowly climbed the stairs, thinking about the story of the Bund Hotel while unconsciously caressing the curved banister with my long fingers. Reaching the elevator floor, I was reluctant to let go of the smooth masterpiece. We reached my floor and departed the elevator, and then Chow stopped and faced me, gesturing to the door of my room.

"Miss Torgeson, these Chinese characters are translated into English as 'Love 9.' All the room numbers in the Bund Hotel are preceded by the word 'love.'"

As I silently absorbed the symbolic meaning, I noticed something in Chow's dark eyes as they met mine, unexpectedly revealing a tender reverence for the hotel's sad history.

He unlocked my room and motioned for me to enter first. I moved under the archway entrance, excited to discover Love 9. The space was elongated with a ten-foot ceiling and was bathed in a soothing green color palette.

Of course—green—the color of the heart chakra. Love...green...heart...Yang Li thought of every symbolic tribute to love.

My eyes rose effortlessly to the echo archway leading to a balcony with a door flanked on both sides by floor-to-ceiling windows. It was a full wall of glass. I walked over and stepped through the arched door and onto the balcony, which was enough space for two chairs. Just beneath me was a splendid garden with mature plants surrounding a fountain in the middle. The intricate garden had obviously been planted long ago and looked as though it was meticulously maintained. I lingered, admiring it, then realized that my room was quiet.

Quickly turning, I saw Chow and the bellman patiently waiting for me.

"I'm sorry. I was admiring the garden," I blurted out, embarrassed.

Chow smiled sincerely in reply, "Of course, Miss Torgeson. Would you like your luggage unpacked?"

"Oh, no thank you, Mr. Lai. I can do that."

"Yes, Miss Torgeson. The bathroom is here," Chow gestured as he opened the door. "Is everything to your satisfaction?"

"Oh, yes. Thank you, Mr. Lai."

Chow spoke to the bellman, handed him a tip, and then followed him into the hallway. He held the door open to speak to me.

"Would you like a wake-up call this evening or tomorrow morning?"

"No, thank you."

"There is a Tai Chi class in the garden tomorrow morning at seven. Would you like to participate?"

"Yes, that sounds like a perfect way to begin my visit here."

"I will arrange this for you. Simply arrive in the lobby tomorrow morning at seven."

"Thank you, Mr. Lai, for everything." I sincerely smiled.

As Chow bowed toward me, he said, "It is my pleasure, Miss Torgeson. In case you need anything, please call my cell at any time. The number is on my card."

"Thank you and good night," I replied, respectfully returning his bow.

As he closed the door, he hooked the Do Not Disturb sign on the knob. I quickly latched the door and exhaled in exhaustion, then immediately kicked off my shoes, stripped off my clothes, leaving everything where it landed, and moved into the bathroom for a hot bath.

As I saw my natural reflection in the bathroom mirror, I noticed the fine lines near the corners of my eyes—smile lines—that hinted at my years. Taking care of my fair skin all these years had paid off, for there was no age showing around my lips, and of course my high cheekbones and heart-shaped face helped defy my age, along with my bob haircut. I was happy to see that I still had no gray among my auburn locks.

The running and yoga is paying off, I told myself.

As I watched the tub fill, I appreciated the simple perfection of the room. The bathroom was a vision of simplicity, adorned in a light-green marble, with a large, deep tub situated perfectly for a relaxing bath, with a view straight out the wide bathroom door to the far archway. Near the sink was a simple decorative bowl with one fresh ivory-colored lotus flower floating within.

As I looked into the bedroom, I admired the majestic carved bed of rosewood claiming the long wall, with two matching nightstands. The wood was a purplish-brown color, richly streaked and grained with layers. Above the center of the king bed hung an enormous, ornate gold and lead crystal chandelier suspended from an even higher ceiling cove, which mimicked the bed size. I was drawn to the headboard, where two beautifully intricate hummingbirds were symmetrically carved, facing one another. I remembered a friend that once explained the Chinese meaning of hummingbirds as "time that stops." As I ran my fingers across the hummingbirds, a lump formed in my throat.

Hearing the water fill in the tub, I checked and found it nearly full and glided into the hot water. It didn't take long to drown any remembrances of my dreadful flight. As soon as I let it all go, I was ready to contemplate sleep.

Standing in my towel in front of the matching rosewood desk, I emptied the contents of my purse, searching for the extra-strength Tylenol. I needed to sleep fourteen hours to throw off my jet lag. I swallowed three pills with a swig from the bottled water.

Tylenol sedated me. No doubt the response was the result of my near suicide when I was sixteen years old. I'd ingested a whole bottle of Tylenol after my mother split up my boyfriend and me. I had every intent of dying that night, having apologized to God for not being stronger and then leaving a note for whoever found me. I took the pills in secret while my parents were on vacation. When I woke up in my bed twenty hours later, I was groggy and realized sadly that I was still alive.

In that moment, two thoughts came to me with perfect clarity.

One—I was not alone.

Two—I had a purpose.

My head pounded, but somehow I recognized that the thoughts had come from somewhere outside myself. I accepted the message, whispering "Okay" as I once again surrendered to unconsciousness.

It was profound how that single event changed my entire life. In that simple moment, I felt that I had an understanding with God, an agreement that I would never voluntarily give up my life again until my purpose on Earth was fulfilled. That knowledge—that there was meaning in my life—was enough for me to choose to be strong from that point forward.

The same Tylenol that I'd used to force an end to my life served now as a valium-like sedative for me when sleep was critical; it was the essence of yin-yang, that everything has its opposite force.

I pulled back the covers and slipped into the soft, fine ivory sheets with my head cradled on the pillow. I was asleep in minutes.

Awaking to the gentle sound of Toshiyke Watanabe's piano on my small iPod speakers, I was grateful to have slept well. I felt rested but could still feel some jet lag weighing me down.

They need to find some way to perfect travel so it's easier on the body. "We should have used all the energy we put into liposuction development into jet lag prevention," I said out loud to the walls.

As I arrived in the lobby, I immediately spotted Chow, who looked perfectly rested and relaxed.

He greeted me with a smile and a bow. "Good morning, Miss Torgeson. May I show you to the Tai Chi class?"

Bowing with a returned smile, I replied, "Good morning, Mr. Lai. Yes, please. Would you be comfortable calling me Ann?"

"Yes, of course. You may call me Chow, if you like."

"Thank you, Chow," I replied with a slight tilt of my head.

I followed him into the same garden that I had seen from my balcony; it was open to the sky. There were beautiful Sakura trees and many layers of green and flowering plants that created an oasis in the center of the courtyard. In the middle was a fountain that splashed the water-loving plants nearby, creating coolness and a soothing sound in the garden.

Chow bowed in greeting to the Tai Chi instructor and spoke to him, then turned to me saying, "Miss Torgeson, this is Mr. Wan, your teacher," clearly using my last name out of respect for me in front of my teacher.

I bowed to Wan, who was at least a foot shorter than me and appeared to be seventy years old, saying, "Good morning."

He responded with a bow, cheerfully replying, "Goo moreing, mees."

I nearly giggled from this un-elderly man's cuteness.

"I will wait in the hotel lobby until you are ready to depart. Enjoy your exercise, Ann," Chow said with a smile, exiting.

When another English-speaking hotel guest joined the class, I smiled and said hello, and then the Tai Chi instruction began. I quickly realized that I would have to watch Mr. Wan and do my best to mimic him, because I simply couldn't understand any of his English. Soon I found my groove in the smooth motions and reached a sense of peaceful contemplation, simultaneously filling with energy. I was breathing deeply and could smell the blossoms nearby. I found myself pondering things from a higher level. It was a new experience for me, and very pleasant.

After class, I bowed to Mr. Wan, thanking him. He beamed.

CHAPTER 5
BELLINGHAM, WASHINGTON
THE YEAR 2012

"What a dream," I said with a start, sitting up in bed.

Oh man—that was vivid.

I had been dreaming like this since I was a child. Sometimes when I awoke, they were so real that I could not tell reality from the dream until a few minutes passed. This particular dream of Shanghai felt real to me. Lulu greeted my exclamations with bottom wagging.

"Morning, girl."

As I sat there petting Lulu, my mind started to get some distance from the dream.

My mind floated back to when my daughter and I had been staying at my aunt's house in Bellingham while my own home was being built.

* * *

I thought about my new house and what I needed to do to get ready to move in. First I needed to make it a safe house.

The network that I was a part of, called GOG, an acronym for Get Out! Government, was an underground organization that operated worldwide. Its mission was to assist citizens around the globe in uniting to fight electronic tracking and government control of citizens. GOG operated off the grid. This was a tight organization, and the only way into membership was by invitation. There were levels inside the organization—to keep it underground—and only someone from a higher loyalty level could invite someone new in. I had been a member of GOG for many years, along with my husband, before he died. I joined to try to help restore individual freedoms to Americans.

GOG was run by a board of twelve people in three physical locations that were secret from every GOG member, except the twelve board members. Messages were ferried by runners who traveled from country to country. A requirement of membership was that the person had to be gainfully employed with some sort of profession or trade. No job-hoppers, underemployed people, or anarchists were ever invited to be members. GOG believed that all its associates needed to be productive members of their communities and governments, so that change could be permeated at all levels. There were rules to follow in membership.

None of my friends or family knew that I was a member of the organization, not even my daughter. Because of Elinor, I was very careful of the jobs I did for GOG, and they knew that I was limited because of her.

Phone contact with other members could be made, but only with throwaway phones provided by the organization. No electronic communication was allowed. In order to locate an alternative repairman, I left a message with a phone number I memorized, using the code name I was given when I joined the movement.

"B40 for Sim, soon," I said, leaving the message.

I then pulled the phone apart, crushed it with my foot, dipped it in a bucket of water, and drove to a public garbage can and dumped it.

Every communication in GOG was coded and memorized. If you couldn't memorize the codes, you weren't given membership. B40 was my code name, Sim was the designation for a SmartWired job, and "soon" meant that I needed the job done in the next forty-eight hours. The organization knew where I lived, and therefore, no further communication was necessary.

At my aunt Saundra's insistence, Elinor and I had moved in temporarily with her when we moved to Bellingham, since her husband had passed away in an accident only a year before, and she had a large house with only her living there. After closing on the new house and before Elinor and I moved in, I'd planned to stay there alone for a few days, leaving Elinor at Aunt Saundra's so that I could keep a lookout for the alternative repairman who was coming to work on the new house.

When he arrived, I would have to give him the code name for our area, and he would have to give me one in return. Every code name was particular to each geographical region. Both people would have to know the region's code before they could communicate within the GOG network. The day after I left my voice message, a man showed up at my new door. I had seen his van pull up the driveway; he had Washington plates on his vehicle.

"Tulips," I whispered to the six-foot, stocky man with short, sandy-blond hair, tanned skin, and a sculpted chin. He looked to be about fifty.

Lulu barked.

"Skagit," he responded quietly.

I gestured to invite him into the house.

"Joe," he offered with a smile.

"Hi," I greeted him, smiling in response.

"Shield too?" he asked, bending down to let Lulu smell him.

"Yeah. Everything. How much?"

"Ten," he answered matter-of-factly, petting Lulu, who was obviously reveling in the attention.

"Okay. Over there," I agreed, motioning toward the home's SmartWired computer.

I handed Joe a slip of paper, and he read it.

Name: Sinéad
Password: SNL10-3-1992

"You're funny." He smiled, looking up at me. "Was that the date?"

"Yes," I replied with a smile. Wow—I guess he got it. I was surprised that he made the connection to Sinéad O'Connor's infamous Saturday Night Live performance.

I went to my purse where I had been holding fifteen thousand dollars in cash, prepared for a hefty fee to have the work done, and retrieved it.

"Extra for the parents," I said, handing Joe the money. The extra five thousand was for GOG. GOG members often referred to the organization as "the family" or "the parents" to avoid using the name GOG.

The organization was operational because of gifts like this from its members. Part of membership was the expectation that the members would financially support the organization. Joe opened the package and fanned through the 150 hundred-dollar bills.

"Thank you," he said, gratitude in his voice as he put the money in his workbag.

After moving his work van into my garage, Joe removed all chips that sent or received a signal from the SmartWired Company. As he was making the unit sterile, I called SmartWired and told them that I had just bought the house and that the system was being removed and replaced with another competing system. It seemed that the customer service entity, a computer, actually sounded smug when I told it that I was replacing the system. My emotions begged me to hang up, but my common sense prevailed, knowing that my hang-up would be tracked in a database that the government would have easy access to.

During the four days that Joe worked at my house, he installed an electronic privacy shield in all external walls of the house. It employed powerful magnet technology to protect my privacy from any technology peekers who targeted my house or me. Peekers could be any number of people: government, hackers, or just nosy neighbors with the right equipment bought through the Internet. I took my privacy, electronic and otherwise, seriously. I was happy when the project was finished and we could speak openly.

"I brought dinner," I announced as I came in the door, the front door automatically closing behind me.

"Good; I'm starved," Joe eagerly responded.

"There's nothing like a delayed friendship to spurn the appetite," I joked, making fun of the fact that we couldn't get to know each other until we had the house safe from peekers.

He smiled.

"I'm gonna make you one of my specialties while we talk."

"What is it?"

"Chicken Piccata, pasta with alfredo sauce, and fresh Italian bread."

"It looks like you brought way more than that."

"I haven't moved in yet, so I had to bring everything to cook with. There's more in the car," I explained, smiling.

"Let me get it," Joe offered.

"That's okay, I've got it."

While I started to prepare the food, Joe continued to clean up the house from his drywall patching.

"Joe, food's ready," I called to him.

"Good. It smells good. Let me just wash my hands."

We dished up and then sat on the floor to eat, since there was no furniture in the house yet.

"This is delicious, Ann."

"Thanks. It's strange to hear you say my name."

"It's the job, not me."

"I know. It's okay."

"It's comfort food, isn't it?" he asked.

"Yeah—and a good ice-breaker, wouldn't you say?"

He smiled and nodded. "Well you're all set here. Sinéad is ready; I'll show you how to customize her."

"It's okay, I know how; I had one before."

"Okay." He took a few bites from his pasta and then turned to me. "There is some information I need to pass on to you," he said with a serious tone, looking at me.

"What?"

"The parents need your help."

"Anything I can do, I will."

"Funny, that's what they said you'd say," Joe replied, smiling kindly.

"Uh-oh. That means I'm predictable."

"I doubt it."

I smiled. "What do they need?"

"The parents have a candidate in Vancouver. He needs one more field test to ensure we can trust him."

"Vancouver, Washington or Vancouver, Canada?"

"Canada."

"Why would they need me for a job there?"

"They want someone from outside the area to pose as government, to challenge the candidate in a meeting."

"Me? I've never played that role in a job before."

Joe offered more information. "You'll be posing as someone in the Canadian government who's a secret member of GOG. You'll be making contact with the candidate to judge how he acts. You are his test."

"Okay."

"You've played that role before, you know."

I nodded. He didn't pry, but I thought of my time with the CIA.

"Who better than someone who's actually done it?" Joe added.

"That's a good point. I just never even considered it before. It seems like a lifetime ago."

"I know the feeling," he responded, looking intently at me.

I guess there are a lot of us now.

"If they hadn't crossed the line and tried to invade people's lives, tracking human beings like they had, the Patriot Act stealing our individual rights, the IRS overtaxing, local government taking people's homes because of two thousand dollars in back taxes, then none of us would have left them," I hotly muttered.

"I agree," he offered simply.

We were on the same team.

"So the job they want me to do…"

"Details on the paper. Then burn it," he said, handing me an envelope and three throwaway GOG phones.

"Why three?"

"One to call in the job the day of, one for the job itself, and a new spare for you."

"Thanks."

I didn't open the envelope, saving it for later.

"It's a good fire-starter for my first fire," I offered, holding up the envelope.

When we finished eating, we stood to gather the paper plates.

"You have a friend in me, whatever's to come," Joe sincerely offered.

"And me," I responded, looking into his eyes.

It'd been some time since I'd spoken to someone at GOG. With my shield in place and the SmartWired feed cut, my house became my sanctuary—a place I knew would be safe from peekers. It was home.

When Joe left, I opened the envelope.

September 29th
604-555-4424

I knew more details would come later. I looked at the date again. That gives me some time. Reading through the job date and contact number a few more times, I memorized them and then set the envelope and paper on fire in my new fireplace.

Sitting on the floor with my six-inch Kindle Elements wireless computer in my hands, I began to set up preferences for Sinéad—like whether I wanted her to open the garage door when I arrived home or whether I wanted to park in the driveway. When I was finished, I clicked Save, and immediately a voice spoke throughout the house.

"Would you like to take a bath now, Ann?" Sinéad asked in an Irish lilt.

I laughed at Joe's smooth work. An Irish accent, I thought. Nice.

"After I move in," I responded.

"Okay, Ann."

This is gonna be fun. I chuckled.

With Joe gone, I set to work planning the other project I needed to complete before moving in.

It wasn't until the next day that I was able to go to the hardware store to get the supplies I needed. After the trip, I piled them in my bedroom closet.

Kneeling in the closet, I pulled up the carpet and pried out the floorboards that gave me access to the unfinished, unofficial cellar beneath my house. I turned on my flashlight, illuminating the space under the house, then hopped down. The air was slightly cool and moist. The space was about a foot shorter than I was, so I had to stoop. With my head popping up out of the access hole, I dragged down the supplies I bought, then moved them twenty feet, towards the middle of the foundation.

With a flathead screwdriver, I removed the industrial staples that secured the plastic moisture barrier covering the loose earth beneath my house. I retracted the plastic to my pre-designated site. Then I grabbed the shovel and dug a hole that was two feet square. With boards I'd had precisely cut at the hardware store, I constructed a box to line the hole. It felt good, fitting the pieces together, hammering the nails in.

As a final touch, I attached a large, steel gate handle on the cover of the box, for easy access. After checking the fit, it felt snug. Leaning over, I slid the box into the hole, packing dirt into the space between the edges of the hole and the box. I was almost finished.

I went back to the closet and grabbed the bio-encrypted combination safe that I had purchased. Returning to the hole and its newly embedded frame, I carefully stowed the safe inside.

The safe was my back-up box, a safeguard many GOG members installed where they lived. I tossed in a stash of cash I had been holding on to, then placed my homemade cover over the frame.

Standing up, I brushed the dirt from my knees, then covered the site with a padded piece of plastic. As a final step, I took a thick black marker and drew a small X on the sub-flooring of the bottom of the house directly above the safe. Replacing the plastic moisture barrier, I then re-stapled it. I cast my floodlight over my work to make sure nothing looked out of place. Nice job, I confirmed to myself. When I needed it, this hidden strongbox would be a lifesaver.

CHAPTER 6
BELLINGHAM, WASHINGTON
THE YEAR 2012

Elinor and I moved in near the end of September. Though I'd been caught up with unpacking boxes and stocking my kitchen cupboards, GOG and my new assignment were never far from my mind. The twenty-ninth came sooner than I expected.

"Well, let's make the call," I announced to no one.

I went to the homebuilder's safe that came with the house, in the wall of the master bedroom. I dialed in the code and withdrew two of the three throwaway phones that Joe had given me. Phones from GOG always came disassembled in Ziploc bags, with a pair of textured fingerprint-proof gloves. Assembled phones were traceable almost immediately. I put on the gloves and constructed one of the phones, immediately dialing the Vancouver, B.C. number indicated in the note Joe had given me.

"B40 for job, instructions needed," I said, leaving the message.

I hung up the phone. Someone from GOG would get my message and call me at this phone within the next two minutes. If I didn't get a call within that time, then the job was off, and I would destroy the phone. I sat on the edge of my bed, staring at the screen of the phone. I couldn't help but count the seconds as they passed.

It always made me nervous to have a live phone in my possession, even if it was only for a few minutes. The truth was that GOG and all its members were considered enemies of our governments. Most governments considered GOG membership a treasonous act, which was why our organization took such extreme measures to protect the anonymity of its members. The government saw us as a threat, but we saw ourselves as the chance to return America to her roots of "we the people."

American GOG members knew the first amendment by heart, mostly because in recent years, the U.S. Government had violated most of its principles without even attempting to conceal its actions. Ironic as it was, we were fighting for the same rights our forefathers had fought for so many years before: freedom of speech, freedom of the press, the right of the people to peaceably assemble, and the right to petition the government for a redress of grievances.

As I thought about GOG and the reasons I was a member, my phone rang, interrupting my thoughts.

"Yes," I answered.

"Code?" he asked.

"Salmon," I replied.

"Victoria," he confirmed.

We're safe.

"Nine thirty p.m. The Gaslight Brasserie...in the private back room...Newton...walk to the restaurant. Questions on your role?"

"What's Newton?"

"Code to get in."

"Got it," I confirmed.

"Stay safe," he concluded.

We both hung up.

I turned off the phone, pulled it apart, crushed it with my foot, and then tossed it in the bathroom sink and turned on the water. I'd dump it in a public garbage can on my way out.

"Sinéad, give me details about the Gaslight Brasserie in Vancouver."

"The Gaslight Brasserie is a restaurant located at 210 Carrall Street near the city's waterfront, in the Gaslight District. It was established eighteen years ago."

"Stop," I said, halting the stream of information. "What four- and five-star hotels are nearby?"

"There are two four-and-a-half-star hotels within a four-minute drive: the Fairmont Waterfront and the Pan Pacific Hotel, which—"

"Stop."

I was only fifteen when the Pan Pacific Hotel opened, and I remembered that Princess Diana and Prince Charles had visited the same hotel.

"What's the best rate on a single queen or king bed at the Pan Pacific?"

"Two hundred and eighty-nine dollars Canadian, with a harbor and mountain view, king bed."

"Book it for tonight."

"Yes, Ann."

I had no intention of driving back into the U.S. over the Canadian border around midnight. I had done that only one other time, and it was a fantastic mistake. Late at night is when the Tactical Terrorism Team, part of Homeland Security, manages the U.S. border, and they always err on the side of suspicion. A friend of mine, who had been dating a Canadian, came back over the border at one a.m. on a Saturday, and before she knew it, they had her spread-eagle, face down on the floor inside the facility, insisting she was smuggling something because she came over the border so frequently. When she tried to explain that she was dating a Canadian, the interrogator screamed, "Shut up!"

Those are not people you screw with, I told myself. *I'll stay at the Pan Pacific.*

"Sinéad, tell me about the Pan Pacific Hotel and its vicinity."

Sinéad answered almost instantly. "The Pan Pacific sits on a pier that overlooks the Vancouver harbor in downtown Vancouver. The Coastal Mountain Range surrounds the harbor. The rooms themselves are luxurious, with world-class facilities, including a spa with a heated outdoor pool. Pan Pacific's overall service is rated five stars—"

"Stop." I paused. With my reservation made, my next question was superfluous. "Do they have Eggs Benedict and smoked salmon on their room service breakfast menu?"

"Yes, Ann."

Mmm—a nice room that overlooks the water, plus breakfast in bed, I imagined. *What could be better than that?*

I got out my overnight bag and began packing the clothes I would need, and then I threw in my bathing suit, cover-up, and sandals, just in case I wanted to swim some laps in the pool. I added my toiletry case, Kindle Elements, and iPod. I was done packing in ten minutes. After taking one last inventory to make sure I had everything I needed, I stowed my bag in the back seat of my car. I was off.

On my way out of Bellingham, I stopped by a park and dumped the water-laden pieces of the GOG phone, then got on I-5 North. Forty-five minutes later, I was at the Peace Arch crossing. After waiting in line for fifteen minutes, I reached the Canadian border. I pulled up to the border-control booth that had the stop sign. There were electronic sensors facing each side of my car, and once I stopped, a robotic arm immediately swept out under my car.

"Hello," I said once my window was down, handing the Canadian border official my passport.

He was a lean man with a serious face. His dark uniform made him look grimmer as he looked at my passport. "Why are you coming into Canada today?" he asked, looking at me.

"I'm visiting the city."

"Where are you staying?"

"The Pan Pacific Hotel."

Serious-face looked more intently at me.

"How long will you be in Canada?"

"One night."

"Do you have any gifts to leave in Canada?"

"No."

"Are you bringing alcohol or tobacco into Canada?" he droned on.

"No."

"Do you have any weapons, including pepper spray?"

"No," I lied.

He looked at his computer, then turned to me. "Alright then," he said, dismissing me quickly by gesturing with his hand for me to move on. He then turned his attention to his computer.

Slowly, I pulled out of his station, paranoid about keeping the speed limit, considering the two Tasers that I had taped to the underside lip of the back seat.

I made my way up Highway 99, and after fifteen minutes of driving, I started to relax. A few minutes later, I took an exit to find a gas station. While I was stopped, I pulled the Tasers off the underside of my back seat and put them in my purse.

Forty-five minutes later, I pulled into valet parking at the Pan Pacific. It was one p.m.

Taking my purse, I let the valet grab my overnight bag from the back seat, and he followed me in. The lobby was three stories high, filled with a mixture of glass, light, marble, and white columns. It was minimalist in furnishings, but grand in style. It was so vast that a game of basketball could be played in the foyer.

"It looks like your room has been upgraded," the redheaded clerk informed me. "You are now in a suite, but you'll still have a water view."

Sometimes GOG had a way of fixing things like this; I didn't ask why. Thanking the clerk, I confirmed that the outdoor pool was open. Taking my bag from the valet, I tipped him and then made my way to the elevators. My suite was on the twenty-second floor.

After opening the door to my room, I saw through the wide windows the sweeping view west to the Burrard Inlet and the distant North Shore Mountains. It was a perfect day without a cloud in the sky. I could see the islands covered with evergreen trees and imagined their pleasant smell; it made me wish I was on my sailboat taking it all in. The suite was pure luxury, with a tan leather contemporary sofa on a neutral color palette spiked with greenery. Its eight hundred and fifty square feet was covered in marble, with a rug placed by the seating area. Entering the bedroom, I saw that the king-sized bed also faced the water. I smiled at the thought that tomorrow morning I could enjoy my Eggs Benedict while enjoying this view of sea and snow.

I plopped down on the bed, checking its comfort. It passed the test.

Wandering into the bathroom, I expected the ordinaries but hoped for a big tub; I wasn't disappointed. There in the middle of the bathroom sat a tub surrounded by picture windows. I could imagine lying in the hot bathtub, stargazing on a clear night.

Moving to the bedroom, I shed my clothes, unzipped my overnight bag, and retrieved the blue and brown tankini swimsuit. After putting it on, I pulled a cover-up dress over my head and then slipped a pair of sandals on my feet. I grabbed a towel, my Kindle, and the room key and then headed to the elevators. I felt content as I descended. It was a beautiful fall day, the sun was shining and warm, and I was in a foreign country.

I got off the elevator at the eighth floor and headed toward the door to the pool deck. After swiping my room card, I caught my breath once again as I was taken in by the panoramic harbor view and snow-capped mountains. The view extended across the harbor to the city of North Vancouver; to the west was Stanley Park with its majestic forest standing at attention. Surrounding the pool deck was a clear glass partition, which allowed for an unobstructed view while visitors lounged. It was a comfortable seventy-two degrees outside, which was uncharacteristically warm for late September in Vancouver.

There were only three other people on the deck and a man swimming some fast laps in the pool. Taking a lounge chair on the far side, I faced the harbor, where shrubs gave me some privacy. As I lay there gazing into the distance, I noticed a seaplane was starting to take off. I had only seen this once before, when my husband and I were sailing near North Pender Island in the San Juans. I'd forgotten how special it was. The seaplane started off slowly across the water, and then as it increased speed, big splashes started forming on the sides of its pontoons. Soon it lifted off the water and was airborne. I continued to watch the activity in the harbor until I decided to swim some laps, since the pool was now empty.

The laps were invigorating. When I was finished, I bent down to grab the towel from my chair. As I turned around, I bumped into a man and started to apologize.

"I knew it was you," he exclaimed.

In reflex, I pulled up my towel, looked up, and was shocked to find my basement co-worker.

"Paul. What a coincidence," I spat out, wondering what he was doing here.

"What are the chances of us being here at the same time?" he asked, beaming.

"Highly unlikely. Are you following me?" I cautiously teased, trying to ignore my natural instinct toward suspicion.

"Guess I'm busted," he said, his smile showing off his perfect teeth. He winked before going on. "I came up here to meet with a software developer who's doing some design work for us, and since Bennett's paying, I figured I'd stay the night, instead of rushing back."

"I guess you're not my stalker, then," I teased. "Was that you doing laps earlier?"

"Yeah. I can see you're a swimmer, too."

"I love to swim. But your laps were faster than mine. I bet you used to swim competitively," I said, keeping my voice conversational.

"Yeah, in high school and college."

"I only knew you'd been a runner."

"Swimmer, runner, geek. Now you know everything about me."

I laughed. He was funny.

"What do think of this sweltering weather?" I asked.

"I guess seventy degrees is pretty hot for Vancouver."

"Not right after you get out of the heated pool," I said, noticing that he was checking out my backside as I dried off.

"Wanna come sit with me? I'm over there," I said, pointing to the far end of the deck.

"Sure. It's really beautiful, isn't it?" he asked, gesturing to the view.

"Yes. Just before my laps, I saw a seaplane take off. I haven't seen that for a long time; it was cool," I said conversationally as we walked to my spot.

"Have you ever flown in one?" Paul asked me.

"No. Have you?"

"Yeah. About a year ago I took an air tour of Vancouver—"

"Wow. What was it like?" I interrupted excitedly.

Paul explained what it was like to fly in the seaplane and see the islands from the air. After we had chatted for twenty minutes, he asked, "Do you wanna grab an early dinner in Gastown?"

I gave it some thought.

"You know, I'd like that. But on one condition."

"What's that?"

"That it's not a date. We work together, so—"

"Oh, you thought I was asking you out on a date?" he teased.

I smiled in response. "I've never walked around Gastown. Do you know it very well?" I asked, deflecting the subject.

"I took a tour here; it's the best way to see the city, especially if you're alone. How about we meet in the lobby in a half hour? I've got to shower off the saltwater pool and of course blow-dry my hair," Paul said, shaking his blond-covered head.

I smiled at his joke. "Half hour sounds good, because I *do* need to blow-dry my hair."

We got up together and made our way over to the elevator.

Later, I was brushing on mascara while the iron heated. I had only brought the clothes that I'd intended to wear to the meeting later that night, so that was the only choice of what to wear now. I ironed my Patagonia black hemp pants and a blue-gray, button-down-the-front cotton top. Putting on my pants, blouse, and watch, I looked at myself in the full-length mirror.

Adding my Keen walking shoes and some lip gloss, I grabbed my small purse and was off down the hall.

Just in time, I thought in the elevator, realizing I was five minutes late.

Once I stepped out of the elevator and into the lobby, Paul quickly found me.

Good, he's not late.

I really did like to be punctual and didn't like it when others were not. I once had a date with a lawyer, and when he showed up twenty-five minutes late picking me up—without an apology—I decided right then that it would be our last date. Thank goodness we had only seen a movie. When he brought me home, I made for my front door like I was bolting from cannon fire.

"You look great," Paul commented, beaming at me.

Cute.

"So do you," I said, noticing his white cotton shirt and khaki pants with pockets everywhere. "We goin' fishin'?"

"Huh?" he asked, perplexed.

"That's a lot of pockets for dinner in Gastown."

"You never know when you might need extra storage," he offered playfully.

I smiled.

"Ready?" he asked, motioning to the exit.

"Yes."

The doorman opened the door, and we were out of the hotel and onto the cobbled streets.

"So are you gonna be my tour guide of Gastown?" I inquired.

"Nope."

"Aww, come on…" I pleaded as we walked side by side.

He chuckled. "You're not easy to say no to."

"Well that's a good sign, isn't it?" I teased.

Paul smiled and then began to tell me about everything we were seeing. When we got four blocks down from the hotel, we reached Water Street, and Paul stopped at the Gastown steam clock.

"Oh good, it's five till; that's perfect," he exclaimed.

"This clock is powered by an actual steam engine," he began with his tour-guide voice.

"No way," I responded, feigning surprise.

He played along.

"It is. There are only six operating steam clocks in the world. This is one of them. The others are in Japan, a museum in Indiana, two more are here in British Columbia, and there's one in London, England, at the Chelsea Farmer's Market there—"

Just then the clock woke up, interrupting Paul as a crowd suddenly appeared—materializing out of nowhere. Fantastic blasts of steam were released as chimes began to play. The crowd's attention was on the clock as it tooted its little tune. Ending the spectacle was a deep foghorn sound.

"I feel like I've witnessed a piece of history," I remarked.

"Well…I hate to burst your warm-and-fuzzy bubble, but it was actually built in 1977."

I laughed.

We walked on, Paul pointing out old buildings and their place in Gastown's history. We stopped for dinner at Finch's; it was a small French café that reminded me of the small neighborhood cafes in Paris. The café was shaped like a wedge on a Y corner, and we sat near a window. Paul had a baguette filled with Brie, prosciutto, roasted walnuts, and tomato. I also had a baguette, but mine was filled with Brie, avocado, red onion, cucumber, lettuce, and tomato. We sat and talked as we ate. Finally, we walked back to the Pan Pacific. When we got to the hotel elevators, I turned to him.

"Thanks for dinner, and for being my tour guide. I had a really nice time."

"It was my pleasure," he offered sincerely.

"Do you think we can keep our meeting here a secret between us? I really don't want to be the target of office gossip, especially since I'm a new employee at AlterHydro."

"No problem. I can understand that. But just so you know, Ann, I'm pretty good at keeping secrets—"

The elevator opened, interrupting Paul, and people streamed out. I thought I recognized an Asian man who passed by me as he got off the elevator. I turned to get a better look at him but could only see his back. I felt that I knew him, but I couldn't recall from where.

Paul got into the elevator, and I followed him, distracted.

"So I'll see you on Monday," he offered formally.

"Yeah."

We stood in silence.

The elevator opened on his floor, and he got out.

He suddenly turned and held the elevator door, looking at me, and said, "Thanks for going with me, Ann."

"You're welcome…I had fun. Bye," I warmly offered with a little wave of my hand.

He reluctantly removed his hand from the door, and it closed.

I rode up to my floor. I had two hours before the GOG job, enough time to soak in the tub.

CHAPTER 7
BRITISH COLUMBIA, CANADA
THE YEAR 2012

After my bath, I ran the iron over my clothes again and redressed. I left myself twenty minutes to walk to the Gaslight Brasserie, having spotted it during my walk with Paul. I made my way down Cordova and onto Water Street, past the steam clock, and then walked two more blocks and turned right onto Carrall Street. It was only a block down from there.

It was a lively place this Saturday; it looked full from the outside. I headed toward the back, guessing that's where the room was.

I asked a passing waiter, "Can you tell me where the private room is?"

"Right back there. See the guy at the door?" he nodded with his head.

It looked like a door to the bathroom. As I walked closer, I could see that it was marked *Private*. There was a mean-looking man standing outside. A GOG bodyguard, maybe; he looked French.

"Hi," I offered, feeling him out.

"You're expected?" he asked, serious.

"Yes."

"And?" he asked.

I leaned to him. "Newton." I confirmed the passcode.

He offered a forced smile of recognition, then opened the door.

Here goes nothing.

I entered a small room with a single, round wooden table surrounded by chairs. The walls were brick; there were no windows. I could see the pingers.

Pingers were electronic devices that measured manmade energy, like bugs, cell phones, wires, recording devices, cameras, or anything that transmitted or received a signal.

Two of them sat opposite one another against the walls to the left and right of the entrance, drawing an invisible line between them. They created an electronic barrier that everyone would have to pass through before reaching the table.

GOG meetings like this were always conducted sans any electronics; it was for everyone's safety. I carried a purse with my room key and the two Tasers but left everything else in my hotel room. Along the front entrance wall, there was a temporary magnetic privacy shield erected, preventing any peekers from penetrating the meeting. The shields reminded me of the science fair displays I created as a kid in school.

The lighting in the room was very dim. Three people sat at the table—two men and a woman. Nearest me sat the woman. She looked to be in her fifties, with short, curly gray hair and a round face with a ruddy complexion, and she was a bit on the chunky side. Wearing a suit, she looked like an intense, intelligent woman.

She doesn't look GOG. Caution tingled my observations.

They all looked my way. Both men stood as I entered. One was very tall, and one was very short, about five feet. Shorty must have been the candidate—he looked a little eager when he saw me. The tall man was about 6'9" and in his midfifties. He was the spitting image of Tom Chambers, the famous Hall of Fame basketball player.

He had blond hair that was graying a little. He too wore a suit. I forced my mind to order as the Tom Chambers look-alike approached me, bearing a bright smile, his hand outstretched. I crossed the barrier, then shook his hand.

"Welcome," he offered.

"My pleasure," I responded.

In GOG meetings like these, there were no introductions, no names—only a mission. The formal greetings we exchanged were standard, like the best of secret societies.

"Would you like to take a seat?" he offered, smiling at me.

"Thank you," I replied and sat.

With my eyes adjusting to the light, I could now see Shorty better. He looked to be in his sixties and had very bushy eyebrows, beady eyes, and very little hair. He put out his hand for me to shake. I shook it.

The serious woman nodded at me, and I returned her nod. No hand was offered.

"Now that we're all here, would you mind explaining why you're interested in the organization?" the Tom Chambers clone asked Shorty.

Shorty looked back at him, then looked from me to the other woman. He took a slow, deep breath.

"When I was a boy," he began, "my father had a substantial gun collection. He hunted. When we were old enough, Dad taught me and my brother how to hunt." He looked over at the Tom Chambers clone, whom he seemed to feel comfortable with, and, meeting his eyes, went on. "We needed the meat, so it was a practical thing, but it was also something fun we did together. By the time I was twelve, I had my own rifle. Dad spent hours teaching me how to shoot it. My brother and I—we were good with our guns, smart and responsible." Shorty then stared down at the table, his face revealing the memories as he recalled the past. "But then the government started restricting who could own guns. By '77, even though we'd been using guns responsibly our whole lives, we had to get permission from the government to buy them. It was a slap in the face. People like me aren't the people the government should be afraid of, and the people they should be afraid of are going to get their hands on guns whether they're restricted or not."

"So it's because of guns that you're interested in the organization," Tom stated.

"No, not just guns," Shorty replied. "Canada has always been known as a country of liberty—it's our history. I know that I should have a right to bear arms, but the government is now controlling that right. When my dad died, I inherited his gun collection. Then the government informed me that I needed to have each of the guns registered." He paused. "I refused—"

"I can understand that," Tom interrupted.

"I didn't see any reason why I needed to. They were my guns, most of them hunting guns—not handguns—and it's not like I take them everywhere. But it didn't matter to the government. One day, I came home to find Lila, my wife, arguing with the local police, who said they had an order to confiscate all my father's guns. I couldn't believe it—they took every single gun from my house." He looked down at the table, gathering his thoughts. "I hired an attorney to fight the order and get the guns back, but it took too long." Shorty took in another deep breath. "My case wasn't scheduled till four months after they confiscated them. One month before the court date, Lila and I woke up in the middle of the night with intruders in our home. They grabbed us from our bedroom—with Lila screaming—and tied us to our own dining room chairs while they ransacked the house."

He stared at the table again. "They were not professionals. They didn't know what they were doing. One of them said to leave us there. The other said to kill us because we'd seen their faces. In the end, they decided to kill us. I watched Lila die, with no way to help her. Then the men heard sirens. I guess one of our neighbors had called the police after hearing Lila's screams." Shorty looked at me steadily. "I'm not a killer, but if I'd had a gun, I would have been able to defend my wife."

"I'm sorry," I sincerely offered.

Shorty looked at me with grief.

"But it's not just that. Last year, it became law that all passports would contain a Radio Frequency ID chip, including a digital eye scan. If you have a passport, then the Canadian government can track you. This year, the RFID chip was required in all new driver's licenses. If I attend a gun show now, all the government has to do is hold an RFID reader within a few hundred feet of me, and he could identify my presence at those events because my driver's license is in my wallet. Since it's illegal not to have your driver's license with you when driving, it's really not a viable option to leave it at home. All of these things are an invasion of my privacy, my autonomy, and my rights. I was born here—this is *my* country—yet I see Canada following in America's footsteps with the über control of its citizens. What's next? The Patriot Act, Canadian-style? I want to be able to go wherever I want within my own country, for whatever purpose I want, without being tracked by my government. It's my right to do so—not because I want to do something illegal, but because I have a right to my own privacy." Shorty paused, wiping spittle from his lips as he swallowed. He was passionate, eyes alight with indignation.

I thought about how to challenge him. "The government can cut you off at the knees by being a part of this organization—they like to use the word treason," I began.

"They can call it whatever they want. If I don't fight, I think my wife will be very upset with me when I get to the other side," he replied, certain.

"What is it that you want to do about it?" the Tom Chambers clone asked Shorty.

"Anything. I want to do absolutely anything that will fight these bullies and change Canada's future. I have nothing to lose—Lila is dead—my children are grown and have families of their own. My bank account is full, and there is nothing I can think of that I want to spend it on. I have two things that are most dear to me: the memory of my wife and my memory of what this country used to be. I figure I'll do what I can."

"If you're caught being part of this organization, you'll be seen as a terrorist by the Canadian government," I warned him.

"It's a risk that I'm willing to take," he said flatly.

I nodded, more to myself than anyone else in the room. He seemed to understand the consequences.

Pressing him, I tried to see if he would break. "The government has endless legal resources, including the ability to change the law to suit their needs. Can you handle that?"

"I tried fighting them once using the legal process, and they killed Lila."

"*They* killed your wife?" I asked.

"As far as I'm concerned, yes. The feds prevented me from having my gun by my side, where it had been year after year, as protection. If it had still been there, I am confident that my wife would be alive today. The reason I want to be a part of this organization is that I don't believe legal recourse has any chance of changing anything. I *want* to change things, and that's why I'm here."

"The Canadian government is serious about pursuing our organization. Do you think you can keep your emotions in check, in order to accomplish the tasks that you're given?" I asked.

"There was no one, besides Lila, who knew how I felt about what our government was doing to Canada."

Then the woman interrupted, nodding to Shorty. "I've known him for more than thirty years. He's the most decent, honest, and forthright person I've known in those years. His passion is fueled by honest-to-goodness patriotism. He's an idealist, like most of us here. He is worthy to be a member of this organization, which is why we're all here now."

"I have two hundred and six bones in my body, and I will fight the government with all of them," Shorty passionately added.

I like him. It was simply a feeling in my gut. He was right for GOG.

The Tom Chambers clone and I looked at one another, silently agreeing.

Time for me to go. We had pushed him as much as we needed to.

"Thank you," I offered Shorty, along with my hand. He shook it.

I stood and then nodded at Tom Chambers and the woman, turned, and walked out the door. I passed the door guard on the other side of the room and made my way through the restaurant, toward the front door.

Outside the restaurant, I stopped to set my watch to clock the time. I was expected to call into GOG by phone exactly thirty minutes after I left the meeting. I set my watch alarm to go off in twenty-five minutes, to make sure I got back to the hotel to retrieve a safe phone.

As I left the Gaslight Brasserie, I breathed in the night air. Listening to the passion of a new GOG candidate was exciting. Here he was, literally willing to risk his life for his country. I'd call him a patriot, and yet his own country would call him a terrorist, a coward. He was a hero in my mind.

I gazed at the full moon, leisurely walking back toward the Pan Pacific. Full moons were always special to me; they had marked some of the most important events of my life. I people-watched as I walked, seeing couples connect, talk, and laugh. It was life.

Two blocks from the hotel, something from the corner of my vision got my attention. Then I heard it—two car doors slamming at the same time.

Casually, I looked to the side, verifying my suspicion. Two men in intelligence-issue black suits had gotten out of a black SUV and were following me.

Oh crap.

As I picked up my pace, so did they.

Who alerted the Canadian authorities? The woman? I considered my options. I didn't know anyone that I could trust in Canada. I did have GOG's local contact number, but the safe phones were still in my hotel room.

Please don't make me fight you, I silently warned the men.

Pulling a Taser from my purse, I looped the strap around my wrist and armed it.

I remembered the Gastown steam clock and how the crowd suddenly gathered. I looked at my watch. Two minutes till the hour. Turning the corner, I sprinted toward the clock as fast as my runner's body would take me. As I did so, I turned to see if they were pursuing me. I saw one man run toward me, while the other ran back to the SUV.

Reaching the steam clock, I saw the crowd gathered. I stooped down lower than the height of the crowd, hiding, then quickly made my way through the crowd, hunched over as the steam erupted.

Once on the other side of the crowd, I took off running as fast I could on Cambie Street, heading toward the Vancouver harbor as I heard the whistles signaling the end of the clock's display. I knew that direction was my only choice if I were going to lose my pursuers. As Cambie Street ended, I turned east, sprinting behind the shops that lined Water Street. Looking back, I didn't see any agents. I figured that I had about a mile or so to run before I reached the cutoff toward the waterfront, which would take me to Portside Park. I knew that I could run in an all-out sprint for that distance.

I reached Carall Street and ran smack into one of the agents. He grabbed me by the wrist that my Taser hung from, pulling the Taser loose.

"You're quite the runner, Ann," he snarled, painfully twisting my wrist.

He knows my name.

I did the only thing I could. I put him down like the CIA trained me to. While he held my right wrist with his right hand, I turned so that my left side was toward his front, picked up my left leg, and stomped down on his right knee as hard as I could.

He screamed in agony and bent forward, spontaneously letting go of my wrist, freeing me. I immediately stepped away, turned a full one hundred eighty degrees so that I was facing the other direction, leaned at an angle, lifted my right leg, and delivered a lean-away sidekick to his face as he was bent over. He face-planted into the ground with a grunt.

"Betcha didn't think I could do that," I exclaimed.

I looked around for witnesses and to see if his buddy had arrived. It was all clear.

The man was unconscious. With my adrenaline in overdrive, I quickly picked up my purse and Taser. I ran full-on toward Portside Park. When I reached the cutoff road leading to the waterfront, a black SUV slammed on its brakes to cut me off, nearly running me over in the process. Out of reflex, I braced myself against the hood to absorb the shock, jamming my wrist in the process, but I still stood. As fast as I could, I flipped the Taser on.

"Get in," a man demanded from the driver's seat.

I turned to run away.

"Ann, it is Chow. Get in."

I looked at him in shock.

"Ann, they are going to be here very soon. Get in the car so I can get you to safety," he urged.

"How do I know you're not with them?" I spat out. *And how is it that you're here, in front of me, when the only other time I've seen you was in a dream?*

"In our dream, you stayed in the Bund Hotel, room Love 9," Chow offered.

My mind was reeling. Was it him that I saw at the Pan Pacific, getting out of the elevator? "Tell me what I did the first morning I was there," I demanded, trying to confirm it was really Chow Lai.

"The Tai Chi class," he answered impatiently, his voice sharp.

I got in the SUV.

"How are you here now?" I asked.

"We cannot talk here."

I sat quietly as Chow sped away, my mind turning over the possibilities. After turning off the Taser, I put it back in my purse, thinking all the while. *How is he here now?* I looked over at him as he drove; it was definitely Chow. We drove for a few minutes, heading back toward my hotel, and then he spoke.

"I will park in the hotel's garage and then get your things from the room and bring them down. While I am gone, use a safe phone from the glove compartment to call the valet and tell him to bring your car to the entrance of the garage. Tell him you are meeting a friend there. Wait a couple of minutes, then call the front desk and check out of your room. That will give me enough time to get in your room while the key works. We need to get you out of here tonight."

"My room number is—"

"I know what room it is," Chow interrupted.

You do?

"When I return, I will see you to your car. Head for the Peace Arch crossing back into the States. Go the speed limit, but get there as quickly as you can. You need to get over the border *now*. And leave the Taser in my car—I don't want you going through border patrol with weapons."

I nodded. "I have questions, Chow."

"I know. But not now—another time," he said gently, promise in his voice as he looked over at me with his dark, penetrating eyes.

I needed my questions answered and didn't want to wait, but I could see the situation was precarious.

A minute later, Chow pulled into the hotel's parking garage. I immediately pulled a phone out of the glove compartment and started to assemble it. Chow got out of the car as soon as he had stopped; he left the engine running. I made the calls and destroyed the phone. I then put both of my Tasers on the driver's seat. I carefully looked at my wrist to see if I had broken any bones when I jammed it on the car hood.

As I felt the bones intact, my watch alarm went off, reminding me to call GOG. I turned it off, and as I looked up, I saw that a black SUV had blocked me in from behind.

Oh no.

I tried to open my door to escape, but instead, my second pursuer yanked the door open for me.

You're new.

With my left hand, I quickly reached over and grabbed a Taser while arming it. I shoved it into the curve of the suit's neck. He crumpled to the ground beside my open door.

One down.

By then my previous assailant was opening the driver's side door, and he grabbed my other Taser before I could. He lunged at me with the Taser over the driver's seat, but I was able to jump out my open door and over the new agent's limp body before he could try to zap me. I sprinted away from the SUV, my pursuer just behind me.

Chow suddenly appeared, charging from the other direction, and landed a three-hundred-sixty-degree jumping spinning back kick into my pursuer's face. The agent was down for the count before he hit the pavement.

The suit had two face-plants in one day. I didn't feel a bit sorry for him.

"What was that?" I hollered at Chow in awe.

"Soo Bahk Do," he confidently replied.

"Incredible," I responded with an adrenaline-charged smile.

I had only seen that move a few times before, from my CIA hand-to-hand combat instructor, but I hadn't seen it since. It was a remarkable maneuver.

"We must get you on your way, Ann," he said, matter of fact.

From the driver's side, Chow reached over into the glove compartment and handed me a plastic bag with another safe phone enclosed.

"Just in case," he cautioned.

"Thank you."

"You'd better get going," he said, walking to where he had dumped my overnight bag, then handing it to me.

"I see my car."

"Then it is time for us to part ways."

I stopped and faced him, so many unasked questions on my lips.

"We will meet again, Ann, and next time I will answer your questions," he said, looking intensely into my eyes.

"I look forward to it," I answered directly.

Chow turned back to deal with the agents.

I tipped the valet and got in the car. I didn't have any difficulty crossing back over the border into America. Apparently the Canadian and U.S. borders weren't sharing computer notes.

In my drive through the dark Bellingham night, I thought about Chow. He was real. And not only was he real, but he was GOG. I wondered what else from my dream was real.

I walked to the front door of my house and sighed a huge breath of relief to be in my safe home. I took a late bath so I could calm myself for sleep.

CHAPTER 8
SHANGHAI, CHINA
THE YEAR 2015

I showered at the Bund Hotel and was meeting Chow in the lobby, to be driven to the Yuyuan Garden, three kilometers from the hotel. On my first full day in China, I was excited to see the four-hundred-year-old classical Chinese gardens in Old Town Shanghai.

We arrived at the garden just as it opened. Chow led me to the gate and paid for our entry. We approached the glorious Eden, restored to its original splendor only two years before, after having been neglected for many years. The name of the garden meant *garden of peace and comfort*, a fitting sentiment from what I observed from the exterior.

Mr. Pan Yunduan started designing the garden in 1559 and continued constructing it for twenty years. He built it to impress his father, who was a high-ranking officer at the end of the Ming Dynasty. The outer and inner garden covered five acres; within these were six distinct rooms. The fact that the garden was far older than many structures in America excited me. We started out walking slowly in a clockwise direction and came upon the Sansui Tang, which meant *three ears of corn hall.*

"Ann, you can see the wood beam carvings of rice, millet, wheat, and fruit here. They are all emblems of a plentiful harvest," Chow explained.

"Beautiful," I whispered.

"This building was used to proclaim royal announcements centuries ago."

I smiled at Chow, imagining such an event.

Walking on slowly, we lingered a while in the Da Jia Shan, where two thousand tons of rare yellow stones had been dramatically sculpted into natural shapes by the famous garden artist of the Ming Dynasty, Zhang Nanyang. Using rice glue, he created mountain-like sculptures, which simulated views of peaks, ravines, caves, and ridges. The sculptures were surrounded by ponds and streams, which contained carp and goldfish. The streams journeyed from one room to the next, connecting the garden. Walking through it was like a journey of time filled with energy.

Chow delicately interrupted what had been a long silence as we walked. "Ann, we are entering the Pavilion of Ten Thousand Flowers. You may wish to know that contained within this courtyard is a ginkgo tree that was planted four centuries ago." He gestured to the tree.

I looked at Chow and sat down on the large carved bench near the magnificent ancient tree. He stood next to me, his hands behind his back, sensing my reverence.

Four centuries old, I thought. *It must be more than one hundred feet high.*

"The ginkgo tree is one of the oldest living species on the earth," he explained.

"I love old trees. They are the true survivors and witnesses of history."

Chow looked at me suddenly and nodded. He seemed surprised by my comment.

"This tree offers life-giving leaves that increase blood flow to the brain through the drinking of its tea."

"And it's fitting that the leaves are yellow," I said, "which symbolizes the third energy chakra of the body."

Startled, Chow answered, "Yes. You are correct." He then smiled at me with his perfect white teeth.

I continued to admire the old tree, feeling a reverence in its presence. Suddenly I felt overcome with emotion that I didn't understand. It was then that I noticed something shining into my eyes from the ground. It was sparkling, as if beckoning me. I bent down to discover the source and picked up a natural crystal. It was three inches, point to point, and sparkling clear to the eye.

"It can't be," I whispered suddenly as I stood.

Realizing that I had spoken out loud, I censored my spoken voice.

Could it be, after all this time? Here, in this place?

Chow watched me curiously.

"When I was a small child, my dad taught me about the earth. We went rock hounding, looking for unique rocks and minerals. He taught me about their healing properties and their influence on the chakras of the body," I explained, still examining the crystal. I looked at Chow.

He nodded. "Chakras. They connect to physical, emotional, mental, and spiritual health. The Chinese have been using minerals to balance the chakras of the body for thousands of years."

I nodded. "One summer, when I was seven years old, my father took me on a trip to upstate New York, where we went rock hounding at a place called Little Falls. We were there to find Herkimer diamonds, which are a special kind of quartz crystal found there. They have six sides, eighteen facets, and two pointy ends called double terminations—instead of one flat end and one pointed end." I paused, recalling what my father had told me. Chow listened intently, watching me with the stone.

"They were believed to have been formed five hundred million years ago," I continued reverently. "They developed beneath the sea as deposits, free-floating in pockets of clay rather than on the side of a stone, allowing for energy to flow through the crystals in both directions. In the clay, they were aligned perfectly with the earth's magnetic field. My dad told me that Herkimer diamonds are used to open the crown chakra, which is the key to one's soul. The Herkimer will clear blockages in the other six chakras, and it can raise a person's spiritual energy level. My dad explained that this particular crystal will allow a person to discover their higher purpose."

"I think that to find this crystal today is good luck for you."

I looked away from the crystal in my hands and into Chow's eyes. "Chow," I quietly explained, "my father and I only uncovered two Herkimer diamonds during our visit. The two that we found were very special—they were both phantom Herkimer diamonds." I held my hand open to show him. "The phantom is shaped when one crystal is formed, and then another is formed around it, to create a mirror image."

Pausing, I watched for Chow's understanding. He nodded.

"It's extremely rare to find one, yet that day we found two, and they were exactly alike, both three inches long. My dad kept one, and I kept the other. We wore them around our necks. Exactly a year later, I lost mine and never found it again."

I breathed deeply, remembering the details of my childhood trip and of the waterfalls near where we found the Herkimer crystals. I looked again at the crystal in my hand, and out of the corner of my eye, I noticed a man standing to the right of me, about fifty feet away. I turned to look more closely at him, but when I looked up, he had vanished. It was the oddest feeling. I looked down at the Herkimer again.

"My father wore his crystal until he died, and he was buried with it around his neck. Chow, I *know* this is the phantom that I lost when I was eight. I know this crystal. I spent hours staring at it. I know its peculiar markings. It's like a part of my soul. It feels the same, and I am transported back to that day with my dad. I feel the same pure spiritual energy that I did that day when I found it."

Chow was silent for a moment, and then he nodded. "Ann, I think you were meant to find this today, next to this four-hundred-year-old tree. That is good fortune."

"I believe you're right," I replied, smiling at him with gratitude that he hadn't doubted me.

Here, in this place, Dad. I felt like he was very close. *I found it. I actually found it.*

My mind went back to those days with my father.

When I was little, I always wanted to be with my dad. It didn't matter to me what he was doing; I just wanted to go along. He once built a television set from parts in our garage, and I was right beside him, watching and learning, handing him tools. Watching him melt the solder was like magic to me. It fascinated me how he could connect wires together in a puddle of melted silver. Each time, the hot soldering iron melted the flux of the wires in a puff of smoke. It was a clear scent—chemical and sharp—but somehow still comforting because I was with my dad. He liked teaching me; it gave him pride to know that his daughter wanted to learn from him, especially since none of my sisters wanted to get their hands dirty or do boy things.

As I stood there, I pondered my relationship with him. He was an important part of who I'd become.

My dad taught me how to tie flies and then how to fly fish in the streams of Washington State. Sometimes on Saturdays in summer, we would wake up at three a.m., and while I packed the car with fishing gear, my dad would brew coffee to fill his thermos and make me a thermos of hot chocolate. Together, we carried out this ritual, driving three hours just to fish for salmon in the Toutle River. We would drive the first hour in complete silence, waking up slowly. Then Dad would start talking about fly fishing, revealing his deep love for the art of it. He told me about how he made his first fly-fishing pole, after his own father explained it to him. He talked about the balance of the pole and how it was an extension of your own arm, and he explained how fly fishing in the middle of a river was spiritual. On those trips, he taught me about listening to my intuition and to the signs that nature itself presented to me. He was not a religious man, but he honored nature. Dad believed in the power of the universe, Chi—the life force—and that one person could change the world.

When we would finally arrive at our self-made parking space in the forest, I would put on my fishing vest while Dad put on his hip-high wading boots. I'd saved up money from walking the neighbor's dog to buy my fishing vest, to which I attached my hand-made flies. I always had a Jon-E hand warmer in one pocket of that vest.

After he geared up, Dad would lock up our 1962 Dodge van, look me in the eyes, and say, “Are you ready?”

I would reply with a smile, “Ready, Dad.”

From then on, we wouldn’t speak again until our lunch break. He led the way through the brush to the river's edge. I then set out on my own to find a good fishing spot, and Dad would wade into the stream. As we breathed in the crisp, fresh mountain air, we would listen to the soft gurgling sounds of the stream. The stream would talk to us as we cleared our minds. We felt at one with nature. It was our mutual goal to find our Chi within the roar of the Toutle River, and we often did. Those were perfect childhood moments.

Now all these years later, standing in front of the ginkgo tree with the Herkimer in my hand, I felt a symbiotic relationship between my spirit and mind and a blending of my past with my present and my future. I felt lighter somehow. It was an otherworldly feeling.

The energy between Chow and I also shifted after I found the Herkimer.

We continued through the garden, walking along the Bridge of Nine Turnings that zigzagged across the lake. *It's kind of like the challenges of life, twisting and turning, trying to make it through.*

Toward the end of the garden tour, we stopped at the lotus pond. I was in awe of the treasure found in this garden.

We'd spent two hours in the Yuyuan Gardens. I was ready for a late breakfast and then, later, my meeting for that day.

During the thirty-minute drive to the factory, I stared intently through the tinted windows, watching all of the people as we passed by. I saw bicycles that looked like antiques from the 1960s, as well as high-tech electric mopeds. It was a convergence of the past with the present.

When we arrived at the factory, I observed four men standing outside the factory door, dressed in suits and looking directly at my car.

"I called ahead to alert the factory of our arrival," Chow explained before he exited the car.

He opened my door and extended his hand to assist me out of the car and onto the bustling sidewalk. I straightened my caramel-colored linen skirt and walked toward our greeting committee. One man bowed and simultaneously offered his business card to me; he was the owner of the factory.

"Good morning, Mr. Zhang. My name is Ann Torgeson," I offered, returning his bow.

Down the line, Zhang introduced me to his managers. It was helpful to have Chow interpret, because other than the owner, no one else was fluent in English, and my Easy Chinese Translations book that I had previously studied was of no help whatsoever.

When I stopped in front of worker stations during the tour, many of the employees looked up from what they were doing and took a short moment to greet me. They seemed like a friendly, kind-hearted people, though formal in the beginning.

After the tour, meetings followed, and we discussed the manufacturing challenges of the turbines. I brought up the planned inspections of the factory by an independent company and conveyed Edwin's expectations of quality assurance.

"Miss Torgeson, would you please join me for an early dinner?" asked Zhang as we finished the last meeting.

"I would be honored, Mr. Zhang. I would like to use my car and driver, if you please."

"As you wish," he replied formally.

When we entered the restaurant, the hostess quickly recognized Zhang. She motioned quietly to another woman, who saw him and led us to our table. As we walked to the far side of the restaurant, I noticed many of the waiters glancing at Zhang and quickly standing a little straighter, heads a little higher. They bowed slightly as we passed. All of a sudden, a bustle began among the workers, treating him as though he were a rock star.

What's that about?

As I passed the enormous fish tank filled with live exotics, I felt a little nauseous to realize that some of the patrons there would be eating the fish in the tank that very evening. I swallowed hard.

At least two-thirds of all large predator fish—cod, bluefin tuna, swordfish, and grouper—in the ocean were overfished and endangered. Chinese fishermen had to go farther and deeper to catch enough fish to satisfy Chinese aquatic appetites. Since there were so few large fish, the Chinese had replaced them with exotics, taking them from the reefs.

It was a long dinner. I was thankful for the late breakfast I'd eaten before Chow brought me to the factory. Even though Zhang ordered several exotics, I focused on discussing business with him, so that I could avoid eating. I knew I'd have to try a few samples to avoid insulting him, but after the obligatory taste, I mostly just rearranged the food on my plate to make it look like I was eating. In the restaurant atmosphere, Zhang relaxed and gave me additional background information regarding the turbine component his company was manufacturing. I made several mental notes that would assist me in writing the technical manual more accurately.

"Mr. Zhang, thank you for dinner," I said during a break in the conversation. "I'm suffering from a bit of jet lag, which is affecting my appetite. As you know, I just flew in from Seattle last night."

"Miss Torgeson, the staff here can help you," Zhang replied fervently as he signaled urgently to the waitress nearby. He said something in Chinese to her, and she scurried off.

"Miss Torgeson, you will drink some tea that will make you feel better."

"Thank you, Mr. Zhang. I'm grateful," I replied with a forced smile, having no idea what was coming.

A waitress quickly arrived with a strong-scented pot of herbal tea. She began to pour me a cup. "It good—drink—Chi balance," the beautiful woman encouraged.

"Thank you," I said, nodding to her.

It's karma. Lying equals bitter tea.

I drank it, then forced a smile at Zhang.

"It tastes like horse piss, but it will cure your jet lag, Miss Torgeson," he informed me.

I would have laughed at his candor, had the tea not tasted just as he said.

After dinner, Chow returned Zhang to his factory, and I thanked the manufacturing president for a productive day.

On the return trip to my hotel, I was surprised to feel my jet lag start to ease away.

That evening, I sat on my balcony in the humid night air, fiddling with the Herkimer in my hand. As I looked at the garden below, I pondered what my father had said about crystals resonating energy: Herkimers cleared the way for a higher spiritual understanding.

As I considered it, I heard church bells nearby start to ring.

I looked out beyond the courtyard to the lights of Shanghai and tightened my hold of the Herkimer. As the roar erupted, I screamed as the hotel began to shake violently.

CHAPTER 9
BELLINGHAM, WASHINGTON
THE YEAR 2015

I opened my eyes and stared at the ceiling of my bedroom at home, trying to piece the dream together. It had been so vivid, so real.

Chow.

My mind reached back…and then I knew. This was a continuation of a dream I'd had three years before.

"Sinéad, what day of the week is it?" I asked, trying to gain my bearings in time.

"It's Saturday, Ann."

"At least it's the day I thought it was," I said, comforting myself. "Give me the first three news highlights."

"First, 8.9-magnitude earthquake levels much of Shanghai city. Second—"

"Stop, Sinéad!" I commanded, gasping in horror.

"Oh no…no…no…it's not possible. No way," I exclaimed in shock, bolting up in my bed.

"Sinéad," I said. "Find the Bund Garden Hotel in Shanghai. Is it still standing?" I asked, anxious.

"No, Ann. The earthquake's epicenter was latitude N 31° 14' 10.7712, and longitude E 121° 29' 9.9126, the same coordinates as the Bund Hotel. Nothing remains."

My mind was racing. *Why would I dream an earthquake that was happening in China?*

"Sinéad, turn on the lights."

I saw a light reflecting off the bed sheet as the lights came on. As I turned my head, I could see the Herkimer diamond. I picked it up in reflex.

I brought it back from my dream? I thought in disbelief.

As I held it, my mind raced back to my husband and what he had said.

"The Herkimer. Believe…"

We had traveled to Bellingham on vacation in 2011 to visit with my aunt Saundra and ski at Mount Baker. Elinor was fourteen years old and wanted to learn to ski. Mount Baker had received six hundred and ninety inches of new snow before we'd arrived to ski that spring. Armond wanted to ski the backcountry of the White Salmon area, while I would go with Elinor as she took her first skiing lesson in the Heather Meadows area. We bought Armond's backcountry permit, our lift tickets, and Elinor's lesson through the website, then the three of us headed to the mountain to play for the day.

As we pulled into the parking lot of White Salmon, I felt a sense of nervousness in my gut. I was always uneasy when Armond skied the backcountry, but since I'd given him an avalanche safety beacon this past Christmas, I had hoped it would calm my nerves. It didn't. Armond dressed in his ski clothes in the SUV.

"You're gonna have good skiing today, Daddy," Elinor gushed.

"I can see that. The powder should be fantastic," Armond said passionately.

"What's that noise?" I asked.

We all stopped and listened.

"Oh, that's the avalanche control team setting off slides," Armond said after a few seconds. They do that regularly in the wilderness area whenever there's heavy snow. We had twenty-four inches of snow in the past twenty-four hours," he exclaimed with a smile.

"I didn't realize it was that much," I said, a little worried.

"Oh, don't worry, love. Everything will be just fine," he told me, kissing me.

"Besides, Daddy has his beacon, right?"

"I do. Did you know there are over one thousand acres to ski here, Elinor?" he asked.

"No. That's a lot."

"It's a big area, which means that we won't get bored today."

"Are you excited about your lesson, sweetie?" I asked Elinor.

"Yeah. I've wanted to learn how to ski for a long time. But I wanted to learn here, instead of in the East. My friends have been telling me that skiing in powder is a lot better."

"It sure is," Armond remarked. "Skiing in powder is a lot different than skiing in the East. It takes a certain technique, so it's really good that you'll learn in powder," he added.

"Well I know it's gonna be fun," Elinor said excitedly.

"It looks like I'm ready. How do I look?" Armond asked us after he stepped outside, posing like he was a ski model.

Elinor and I laughed and kept laughing harder as Armond posed.

"Daddy, you're so funny."

"I aim to please. Well, you two girls have fun on the bunny slopes. I'll meet up with you at lunchtime in the lodge, like we planned, and then we can ski together for the afternoon."

"Sounds good," I said.

"Now give me hugs," he demanded playfully.

The three of us had a family hug.

"Don't worry," Armond said sternly, pointing his finger at me.

"I'll do my best not to. Love you, baby."

"Love you too," he said, kissing me warmly on the mouth and holding me for a few seconds.

"Love you, Daddy," Elinor offered, while Armond reached down to her for a hug. He then lifted her off her feet.

Elinor laughed.

Armond grabbed his skis off the rooftop carrier and headed to chair lift seven, which would get him to the Shuksan Arm backcountry.

"Daddy's goofy," Elinor said, watching him walk away.

"He is that," I agreed with my arm around her waist, watching Armond.

We got in the car for the short drive to the Heather Meadows area. Elinor and I parked at the upper Heather Meadows parking area, got dressed in the car, and then headed to the lodge for our rental skis. The building was cedar sided, a traditionally styled rustic alpine lodge with three stories. The lodge side facing the ski runs was covered with enormous picture windows down the side, so you could watch the skiers from the warmth of the many stone fireplaces in the lodge. The backdrop of Mt. Shuksan dwarfed the lodge.

"This is one of the prettiest places on Earth, don't you think, Elinor?"

"Oh yes, Mommy."

It was a breathtakingly beautiful day with snow falling; we would need our goggles. We got fitted for our rentals and were joking around with the young staff in the lodge. In the gift shop, Elinor stopped to look at hats.

"What do you think of this one?" she asked me after trying on a blue knitted cap.

"It's just beautiful," I told her.

"Do you think Daddy will like it?"

"Of course."

"Then I'll get it. I want something that I can always look at and remember this day."

Elinor bought her commemorative hat, and we left the shop.

Her class was gathering for the lesson just as we made our way behind the lodge. I showed Elinor how to put on her skis and then left her to her class. As I was walking back to the lodge, my cell phone vibrated in my pocket, playing Nirvana's "Come as You Are," which was my ring tone for Armond's calls. I opened my phone and saw that he had sent me a self-posed picture in the backcountry ski area. He wasn't yet covered with snow, so he was obviously at the top of the ski run. I smiled at the picture. Armond was beaming.

I put the phone back in my jacket pocket and walked over to the big lodge, securing my skis in the public holder outside. I then went in to get some hot chocolate. Fifteen minutes later, cocoa in hand, I walked over to the bunny hill area where Elinor's class was learning how to snow plow. I took out my small camera and snapped pictures of Elinor's first lesson. She was doing pretty well for an awkward fourteen-year-old. A half hour later, my cup was empty, and I walked back over to get my skis, in anticipation of Elinor's hour-long lesson ending. As I dropped my cup into the garbage, my heart felt like it had skipped a beat, and I had to steady myself.

Passing the lodge, I heard some commotion behind me. I then saw a rescue team hastily assembling and heard the words "…caught in an avalanche…."

Turning abruptly, I approached one of the members of the avalanche team.

"Which part of the mountain had the avalanche?" I asked directly.

"Right now all I know is that it's in the wilderness area accessible from White Salmon," the worker quickly answered.

I backed away.

"Are you all right?" the worker asked me.

"My husband's up there," I responded in a numb voice.

"You'd better sit down," she said, seeing my shock.

"I'm okay," I responded, briskly turning to face Elinor's ski class, trying to restrain my mounting panic.

Elinor saw me and waved. I waved back with a forced smile.

I felt sick inside, imagining Armond buried in the snow, my thoughts racing, telling myself that he could still be okay. That niggling sensation redoubled, and then nervousness overcame me.

Standing there, I watched Elinor finish her lesson as my mind reeled. I'd been going over the words in my mind, trying to figure out how to tell her what I already knew in my gut.

It was two hours before they found him. The way he had finally landed after crashing in the surf of the avalanche left him able to breathe, although he was partially buried. The rescue crew said they wouldn't have found him without the beacon he'd been wearing.

I held Elinor by the shoulders as I told her. She cried hard, trying to catch her breath.

The woman who had been updating us regularly approached.

"Ann, can I speak with you?" she asked. It was the seriousness in her eyes that prompted me to take a few steps away from Elinor as we spoke.

"How is he?" I asked her, as she turned me so that my back was to Elinor.

"Armond is about to arrive. He is conscious and asking for you."

"Thank God," I exclaimed.

"I must warn you, Ann, he's critical. He has several fractures and very serious internal injuries."

I couldn't hold back the dam of tears I had successfully kept at bay for Elinor's sake.

"I'm sorry," I blurted to the rescue worker.

"Oh, it's okay. You have every reason to be emotional. You must prepare yourself, though. It's pretty bad," she warned.

Is this it? Is this all I get…all Elinor gets? How can I finish raising her without you? I asked Armond silently.

"Ann, I can keep Elinor with me while you see him," the rescue worker said, interrupting my thoughts.

That, more than anything else she had said, chilled me, numbness creeping into my hands, my legs, my face. "Is he that bad, that she can't see him too?"

"Yes," she said quietly.

"Give me a minute to think," I asked, trying to calm my racing thoughts.

After a minute of silence, I said, "Armond has a Do Not Resuscitate order filed with his doctor. He would want you to know that," I said flatly, trying to let my mind take the lead over my emotions.

"Okay. Just a minute, Ann," she responded with a nod.

She radioed the rescue extraction team.

"Ten-four on the DNR," I heard them confirm by radio.

"I would like you to keep my daughter with you when Armond arrives, but I need to ask you to keep her somewhere close where she can at least see him from a ways off. Okay?" I asked her.

"Yes, of course. I'll do that."

"Let me tell Elinor," I said.

I turned around and walked back to Elinor while the rescue worker followed.

She saw it on my face, eyes widening, and she began to shake her head emphatically. I rushed the last few feet and hugged her hard.

"Oh sweetie, sweetie, my darling," I consoled her.

After a few minutes in our sorrowful embrace, I took Elinor's arms and held her face to face with me. "When Daddy gets here, I'm gonna go over there and see him. You'll stay here with this rescue worker…"

"What's your name?" I turned my head, asking her.

"Cosette."

"Cosette will stay here with you for a few minutes while I see Daddy. Let me see how he is first, okay?"

"No, I want to stay with you, Mommy," Elinor pleaded, small and vulnerable, a little girl again, instead of our awkward teenager.

I hugged her again, holding on, thinking.

"Give me just a minute with Daddy alone, and then Cosette will bring you over, okay?" I asked her.

"Okay, Mommy," she responded, acquiescing.

I kissed her on the forehead once more, then put my cheek to her head, looking over to Cosette in a silent plea to take care of my Elinor.

After releasing her, I rushed over to the staging area after seeing the rescue sled approach.

As the team stopped, they lifted Armond onto the emergency assessment table, where a medical team waited. Armond saw me. Our eyes locked. Around him, the rescuers were quickly relaying vitals to the medical staff, but I only saw my beloved. Without permission, I moved to his head.

"It's okay, babe. I know," I whispered to him, choking the words out through my tears.

"I'm sorry," he labored, with a weak raspy breath.

"Don't you leave!" I pleaded with him. "We haven't had enough time—"

"Love you both," he softly interrupted.

"Don't. Don't. We need you," I begged, realizing he was saying goodbye.

His eyes blazed into mine. As I moved to kiss him, I heard him barely whisper, "The Herkimer. Believe…" My lips grazed his forehead, cold and clammy, and I drew back, but he was gone, eyes staring past and through me, vacant.

Sorrow took control of every cell of my being, and I could only respond with heaving sobs. There was no thought, no language, no time, only tormented wailing that erupted from me as our two souls were torn apart, one in this world, one departing for the next.

The medical team quietly backed away.

I held my husband as Elinor rushed over to us.

I turned to her, crying, "Oh darling, darling. Daddy's gone. He's gone."

"Daddy," she called out, mustering him.

No reply.

With all of the courage that a fourteen-year-old girl could summon, Elinor gathered up her father, kissed him on the forehead, and whispered, "Goodbye, Daddy. Watch over me," as tears fell from her eyes onto his lifeless face, with her new hat perched upon her head.

At that, neither of us could hold back our desperate grief. We sobbed together, holding him until the tears cleansed our minds, replacing thinking with a numb existence.

They called it shock. I suppose it was. I barely remember the drive off the mountain. Cosette was kind enough to take us to Aunt Saundra's house in Bellingham. I guess someone from the rescue team called ahead and prepared my aunt, because when we arrived, she was waiting for us.

"Hi," I softly greeted her at the door with Elinor at my side.

My aunt hugged us both hard, silence buffering her own grief from us.

Finally releasing us, she said, "I'm sure you both need rest. Let's get you upstairs, where I've made up beds for you."

"Thank you, Saundra," I replied.

We solemnly began treading upstairs. I stopped after several steps, and Elinor followed. I turned toward the front door, where Aunt Saundra quietly talked with the relief worker.

"Cosette, thank you," I offered with as much voice as I could summon.

"You're welcome, Ann. I'll think of you both," she responded.

I tried to smile but failed. I broke eye contact with Cosette, looked at my aunt for a moment with nothing else to say, and then turned and continued slowly up the stairs with my arm around Elinor.

"Mommy, I want to sleep with you, okay?" she pleaded softly.

"Of course, sweetie," I replied with empathy, gently kissing the side of her head.

We entered the room at the top of the stairs that seemed ready for us. The sheets were turned down on the queen bed in the large room, and a vanilla candle was burning on the dresser.

I appreciated my aunt's kind gesture. Seeing the candle, Elinor turned to me, putting her head on my shoulder.

"It's going to be okay," I whispered, with my arms around her. "We're going to be okay. Daddy will watch over us."

Saundra appeared in the doorway. "I've got some pajamas set out for both of you, from when you stayed here before, so there's no need to worry about anything," she assured us. I was again grateful for her kindness.

"Thank you, Saundra," I responded flatly.

"Do you want some herbal tea?" she asked.

I shook my head.

"I think we'll just sleep," I said, looking around the room.

"Both of you—just tell me anything you need, and I'll get it."

"Tomorrow I'll need to get our things from the rental cottage on the mountain and check out."

"We'll worry about that tomorrow. Just rest yourself now. You can stay with me for as long as you want," she protectively offered.

Both Elinor and I dressed down quickly and dropped into bed like we were unaccustomed to gravity. Exhaustion drew us quickly to sleep.

After sleeping for five hours, I awoke suddenly.

I quietly left the bed, careful not to awaken Elinor, and walked down the hall to my aunt's bedroom. "Saundra?" I whispered quietly.

I had always been very close to my aunt; she was kind and gentle. Besides my husband and daughter, I was closer to her than anyone else.

She slowly awoke from sleep. "What is it, dear?"

"Can you talk for a bit?" I asked.

"Of course. Come snuggle here with me," she said, pulling the bed covers aside.

I lay in the bed with her, with her pillows behind us and Saundra's arm wrapped around me, holding me to her carefully.

"What is it?" she questioned.

"At the end…" I started to softly cry. "Armond said, 'The Herkimer. Believe…'"

"What? What was he talking about?"

"It was as if he was going to say something else, but he didn't have enough time."

"What do you think he was going to say?"

"I don't know. Do you remember when I told you about the Herkimer crystals my dad and I found when I was a girl?"

"Of course I remember them."

"Well, I've been going over it in my mind, and I just don't understand why Armond would mention the Herkimer then. Was he remembering a conversation we had about it, or something else? Those were his last words, and I have no idea what they mean."

"With time, Ann, you'll understand. Have faith in that," she consoled me. "We're not always meant to know right away. Give it time," she offered with a squeeze to my shoulder and a kiss on my forehead.

I snuggled into her and allowed myself to be comforted.

We stayed with Aunt Saundra for two weeks after burying Armond in Bellingham. Since we had both grown up there, it seemed like the right place for him to rest. Even though we had lived in the Washington, D.C. area for a long time, Armond and I had always talked of moving to Bellingham when the right professional situations came up for us both. After the funeral and some time passing, I started to crave being back home again. There was a part of me that was reluctant to leave Armond, but Elinor and I finally flew home on a solemn plane ride, so that we could begin to put the pieces of our life back together. I wondered if I would still feel him near if we flew away, but I had to, for Elinor.

Living without Armond that first year was like living without air. When he was beside me, the very air we breathed seemed alive—it was as if there was more oxygen. He brought everything to life. The void created by his absence was like a black hole, sucking the essence of my life away, no matter how hard I fought against it. I pleaded with God, and He did comfort me. But I knew that I was more of a woman when Armond was alive, and without him, I was simply—less. The broad nothingness never seemed to ease that first year; it only shifted back and forth from my conscious to my subconscious. I tried to live in the present, but I knew that the present could be so much more with him, and I had trouble staying in it. So I dreamed of him. I dreamed of living another life with him at night while I slept.

I couldn't have been who I became without the love that we had shared. It was a short time together—we were married only fourteen years—but it had felt like so much longer than that to me. We were like children, playing and laughing, but then we'd talk into the wee hours of the night about the mysteries of life. When he'd been gone for some time, I came to know loneliness in its earthly form.

Though I knew in my mind that others had felt such loss, this loss was mine, and I felt that no one would ever understand it, and to try to explain the loneliness and pain I felt would be futile. It was a reality that I couldn't share with anyone else. It was agonizing torture to be without my best friend, confidant, lover, and mate. From the day Armond left, Elinor was my only solace.

In the years since his death, I thought that Armond's last words were the beginning of a thought he had about my dad. It never did make sense to me. Could he have known what was to come? Was he so close to death that he could see the future?

"Sinéad," I said, dragging myself from thoughts of the past. "Give me information on the earthquake and talk me through it while I take a bath…warm bathroom…hot bath…start the water now," I instructed, holding tight to the Herkimer rediscovered in my hand.

"Yes, Ann."

I drifted down into the soothing warmth, pouring in eucalyptus oil to induce clarity of mind. As I dipped into my deep bath and snuggled into its warmth, I exhaled the memories.

One of the things that attracted me to buying the house in the first place was this bathroom. The high-tech bathtub sat in the middle of the room, creating an open feeling. The shower was in the far corner, surrounded by clear glass. There was a comfortable chaise lounge to relax on to the left of the tub, where I often lingered. The oasis was designed with the colors of sea-foam green and flat ivory—these were the colors that evoked in me the feelings of protection. Water was my respite, and I could think more clearly when surrounded by it.

"Sinéad, go ahead with the earthquake data, slowly."

As Sinéad began to recite the information, I tried to make sense of the events with my analytical mind. By the end of my bath, the details began to settle. What I still didn't understand, though, was how the Herkimer fit into the story.

CHAPTER 10

BELLINGHAM, WASHINGTON THE YEAR 2015

Michael Gettel was once quoted as saying, "There is always music in the San Juans. Listen closely, and you can hear the splashing seal, otter, and whale. ...it is the heartbeat of the San Juans."

"Play Michael Gettel, San Juan Suite."

"Okay, Ann," Sinéad agreed, queuing the music.

It was this heartbeat of the sea that lulled me into peace through Michael's music. Not long after San Juan Suite was released in 1987, I saw him perform live in a café when my best friend, Jackie, and I were visiting Seattle. Afterwards, Jackie introduced us to Michael, even though she'd never met him before—she was always so bold. I was impressed with Michael's passion for nature and the piano, and how he harmonized the two in San Juan Suite. I found myself flirting with him until Jackie nudged me, bringing me back to reality. We were just sixteen-year-old kids, but I had my first crush on a boy. Jackie was a moral compass for me, and I was alternatively annoyed by and appreciative of her efforts. She taught me a great deal about friendship, kindness, and loyalty. Listening to San Juan

Suite brought back good memories of Jackie. We did have an excessive amount of fun in the years that we were best friends.

With Michael's music resonating throughout the house, my home came alive with the heartbeat of the San Juans. I sat on the window seat as I read my email on my Kindle Elements.

My house was built solely for a view of the sea. It sat on the highest elevation in Fairhaven and had a distant view of the San Juan Islands. Living here, I felt like I could be a part of the sea without actually being on it. The large open den sat on the other side of the living space, facing west, surrounded by a row of bay windows that overlooked Chuckanut Bay. I'd had tile installed in that den and converted the space into a potter's studio. In it were my potter's wheel, a rolling utility cart, and an open cedar bookshelf. The bookshelf was seven feet high and held several pieces of drying pottery. The area was a clean, open space that looked both organized and inviting. Most of its light came from the wall of windows and the three skylights above.

As I sat in the window seat overlooking the sea, I thought about Armond and the political discussions we'd had. I thought about America and the way it had changed in recent years.

Seven years ago was the turning point for America. From the summer of 2008 until 2009, the America I knew and loved fundamentally changed. It started with the American government buying into the largest banking, mortgage, and insurance companies in the country. In 2008, *Time* magazine called America a socialist country, "only with worse food." It stirred up and scared Americans.

I was thirty-seven, and I knew these significant changes were bad for the country. I couldn't shake the uneasy feeling in my gut. Then the stock market nearly crashed and took with it the retirements of many middle-class Americans. Luckily, when the chatter started about the possibility of bailing out AIG, I had a moment of inspiration and cashed out every investment I had. It took a week to receive the checks.

When I went to my bank to cash them for hard currency, the teller objected. Hand in hand with the crash, banks were failing, and there was fear about bank runs. I asked for the branch manager. After introductions by the teller, Paula Myre met with me in her office with the door ajar.

"Miss Torgeson, how can I help you?" she said, chill and professional.

"I want to cash my investment checks."

"You do not want to deposit them?"

"No."

"May I ask why?"

"No," I said, crisp and sure. I owed her no explanation, and I made it clear in my tone.

Paula raised a smug eyebrow; clearly she was used to getting her own way. I waited her out while she looked at me, considering.

"It's really much safer to deposit these checks. It is a large amount."

I wasn't about to debate with her—or give in.

"Why don't you check the balance in my accounts and my history with the bank?" I said, trying to get her to understand that I was a customer worth keeping happy.

I waited while she typed.

"Miss Torgeson, I can see that you have enough here to cover the checks. But I would really prefer that you deposit them."

"No, thank you." I waited again for her next rebuttal but then conceived a counter-attack. "Ms. Myre, is the problem that the bank doesn't have enough money to cash my checks?" I asked in a very loud voice, making sure those just outside the door could hear.

"Oh, no..." she said with a nervous blush, getting up to close her office door. "Absolutely not...the bank is perfectly sound."

"Then why won't you cash my checks?" I questioned her.

"It's not that we don't want to cash your checks."

"Then what is it?" I asked, getting frustrated and now willing to become pushy.

Silence. At least a minute passed as she looked again at her computer screen.

"Well, if you'll just wait a few minutes, I'll get the cash to take care of this for you," she suddenly announced with pursed eyebrows, unwilling to look at me.

"Thank you, Ms. Myre. I'll need that in one-hundred-dollar bills."

"One-hundred-dollar bills? Do you realize that's over eight hundred bills?" Paula said, shock pouring into her voice.

"Yes, I do," I responded, matter of fact, staring her down. "You have an electronic bill counter, right?"

"I don't know if—"

"Are you telling me that you don't have enough cash in the branch?" I repeated, in the same tone.

"We do...we do. Just a moment," she said nervously.

I waited while Paula opened the door, closed it behind her, and disappeared into the vault. Clearly she was trying to keep cash in the bank, no doubt having been coached by her executives.

Paula returned twenty minutes later holding a bag. *Finally*, I thought.

"Eighty-nine thousand dollars is a lot of cash," Paula said again.

"It is. Didn't I do well with my investments?" I said with a smile, ridiculing her.

Paula didn't answer and looked down at my cash. She looked like she swallowed back a snide remark that was brewing in her stomach. After a deep breath, she began to count out the bills from her desk. When Paula was finished, she exhaled loudly but still said nothing. She returned the cash to the bank bag, then handed it to me.

"Did you want security to escort you to your car?" Paula reluctantly offered.

"No, thank you," I responded, putting it into my messenger bag.

I stood and turned to walk out.

"Have a good day, Miss Torgeson," she replied, as though her collar had been starched and was pressing into her throat, choking off the words.

I didn't look back.

I hope I never see you again.

The following week, I went to a different branch of my bank and withdrew all but fifty dollars from my savings and checking accounts. I tried to make my withdrawal through the drive-through window to avoid another teller coup d'état, but I was made to come inside and wait in line. Since my withdrawal was ninety thousand dollars, I did have a déjà vu moment with the second branch manager. I had mentally prepared myself for the dialogue this time. There's nothing like a bank meeting their customer's expectations. It's a good thing that I was withdrawing it all, because the way they behaved made me want to close my accounts anyway.

It was only two weeks after I secured my cash in the safe in my Washington, D.C. townhouse that *Time* magazine, in September

2008, published the article "How we became the United States of France." The article pointed out how we nationalized our financial system and some of the auto companies, how our social security system was going belly-up with baby boomers retiring en-masse, and now there was talk of national health care.

America literally bought the bad debt of financial institutions all across the country, which sent a shock wave through the whole world. The stock market bounced back and forth like a ping-pong ball. Many Americans lost their homes to mortgage foreclosures. A massive recession continued through 2012, even though at one point the government vowed that the USA was recession-free.

After President Obama involved the United States in civil unrest around the world, gasoline prices started to soar. He couldn't seem to do anything right, though it seemed he was trying. Even the glory of his 2011 successful kill order for Osama Bin Laden didn't help his image for long. Behind the scenes in the White House, there were sinister executive orders being signed by him, destroying the individual freedom of Americans. Under the guise of protecting America, Obama supported an RFID chip in every driver's license and government-issued identification in America. By the end of 2012, every American was required to be "chipped" via their government identification. Since it was a federal crime to tamper with a government-issued ID, all Americans could be tracked down at the government's whim, through this ID.

Suddenly I felt a weight pulling me down, thinking about the country's past. "I'm funking out here," I chided myself.

"Sinéad, play my favorites from the Talking Heads, starting with 'Once in a Lifetime.'"

"Okay, Ann."

The lyrics started.

"Louder, Sinéad," I said.

"Okay, Ann," Sinéad responded, raising up the volume a notch.

My head started to bob as I got off the window seat.

"Louder, Sinéad."

"Okay, Ann."

The house came alive with the music bouncing from wall to wall. I could feel the energy pulling me out of my funk.

I started to form a plan to go for a drive out on Chuckanut, following the shoreline of the bay. In my closet, I dressed in a pair of black SecondSkin pants and a generous yellow cotton top that showed a hint of cleavage and touched my middle thigh. I imagined the winding drive in the convertible with the music blasting in the crisp spring air.

Moving to the bathroom, I stood brushing my hair. "Sinéad, what's the weather like for the next two hours, driving south on Chuckanut Drive toward Skagit County?"

"It will be in the midseventies for the first hour, then fifty-two degrees toward the end of the second hour, with clear skies."

I quickly put hair gel in my palm and rubbed my hands together. I ran my hands through my hair, preparing to be windswept. After grabbing a fleece scarf, a zippered sweatshirt, and my purse, I headed out to enjoy the fresh air along the Pacific coast while it was still light. Lulu tried to come along, but I had her stay. She didn't like it when I played loud music in the car, which I intended to do.

"I'll be back very soon," I told her, preparing her Kong ball with peanut butter and dog treats. She would work to get the treats out of it the whole time I was gone.

I slid into the driver's seat, expertly wrapping my scarf around my neck and lowering the top of the BYD at the same time.

"Play Chuckanut Mix, low volume," I said. Heading out of the driveway, I floored the BYD, smiling as I slightly peeled out the tires. Backing off my aggressive driving for the sake of my neighbors, I made my way through the streets, seeking the freedom of Chuckanut Drive. Five minutes later, I was through the city.

"High volume. Start with 'Burning Down the House,'" I commanded the BYD.

While the wind blasted my cares away, I whipped around the curves of my very own freedom road, accompanied by the Talking Heads.

CHAPTER 11
BELLINGHAM, WASHINGTON
THE YEAR 2015

I pulled into my garage, leaving the BYD's top down, and walked into the house. After my head-clearing freedom ride, I felt centered and happy. I snuggled into the deep cotton cushions covering the window seat overlooking the sea. On the ledge next to the seat sat a pair of high-powered binoculars, which I used to spot sailboats in the bay. During the months of May through September, I often drove to Sandy Point with those same binoculars to spot Orca whales that fed and frolicked between the islands. Sandy Point was a finger of land, reaching out into the salt water toward Orcas Island in the San Juans. Every time that I successfully found Orcas from that point, joy filled my heart at the beauty of the magnificent place. It was just as Michael Gettel said: the sea is the heartbeat of the San Juans.

In 2012, before I moved from Washington, D.C. to Bellingham, I sold my townhouse in the Adams Morgan neighborhood of the city for nearly four times what Armond and I had paid for it many years before. The sale generated enough cash to allow me to purchase the Bellingham house outright, make the peeker repairs, buy my BYD H12, and still keep a significant amount of savings in my pocket. I also had the cash in my house safe that I had withdrawn from investments and bank accounts in 2008. I didn't owe anyone any money, and for the first time in my life, I was financially flush. However, my Fairhaven neighborhood in Bellingham couldn't even try to compete with the lifeblood of Adams Morgan.

I remembered the Red Sea Ethiopian restaurant, where patrons ate communally—without utensils. I longed for my metropolitan group of friends who accompanied me to the Red Sea once a month. They were an eclectic group and included an artist, a reporter, and a technology nerd. My friends were independent, outside-the-box thinkers who were full of passion. We had lively discussions about everything from politics to art. The Red Sea's food was extraordinary, but the intellectual feast with my friends was even better.

My new Fairhaven neighborhood didn't offer Ethiopian food, but it was a haven where gifted artists could showcase their works in little shops that lined the bricked Main Street. The Main Street reminded me of Georgetown's cobbled streets, and it was that one thing that drew me to the neighborhood when I was house hunting. Bellingham did have one spectacular beauty: its partnership with the sea. It was a harmonious marriage of salmon, seals, Orcas, salt, and wind. With hundreds of islands in the San Juan Archipelago begging for exploration, most people either owned a boat or knew someone who did. Bellingham's soul seemed to exist on the water instead of in the small city itself.

I looked over to my potter's wheel, a wave of creativity buoying me up. I hopped off the window seat and began to set things up.

"Let's just see what I can discover in you today," I told the clay as I kneaded it.

"Sinéad, play a U2 mix, medium volume."

"Okay, Ann."

Using my hands to create ceramics gave me great satisfaction. There were no rules to obey in throwing on the wheel—there was technique to be sure—but no rules. It was in that moment of creation that I felt free. As I immersed myself in the clay, my mind drifted to my husband, Armond, and the life we shared.

He was my soulmate, and it was so clear to the both of us that it was undeniable. Our love affair started before we had ever met. Armond was on a humanitarian mission in São Paulo, Brazil. At the time, I was doing some freelance writing for the *Washington Post* on humanitarian issues in South America. I learned about Armond's work there through a mutual friend, and I began to write to him, asking for details I could include in my article.

In the beginning, it was all in the spirit of journalistic pursuits, until I became impressed with Armond, as a man, through his letters. He wrote with compassion about the struggles of the people he was helping, and he seemed to really want to be a force for good in their lives. He told me of the long hours he worked to help a handful of families rebuild their shanty-like homes after a bad storm. As he tried to better their lives, he also helped them better themselves. "It won't do them any good," he wrote, "to build them new homes and buy them new clothes if they can't learn to support themselves on their own." I was surprised at the openness with which he shared some of the details of his work, but I was gratified that, though he'd never met me, he felt comfortable being open. I'd originally been drawn to him for his apparent generosity, but as we wrote over the course of several weeks, he became real, much more than the story I'd planned to write about. I opened up in response to his candidness and ended up sharing more about my life with him than I'd expected.

At some point, I asked if he would agree to an in-person interview in São Paulo. I was interested in Armond, and I wanted to see if the chemistry I felt as I read his letters would extend to face-to-face interaction. When Armond agreed to the in-person meeting, I booked a flight. The journey to São Paulo was brutal. One of my planes was grounded due to mechanical problems, and I was rerouted through another city, missing my connecting flight. That created a chain of events, with one delay after another. Twenty-seven hours after I departed, I arrived in São Paulo, exhausted. As I stepped off the plane, my fatigue vanished when I saw him.

Armond was standing at the end of the Jetway, six feet tall and fit, wearing hiking boots, knee-length khaki shorts, a worn t-shirt, and a fleece jacket. He had short brown hair, and his steely-gray eyes were framed by round wire-rimmed glasses. I attempted to contain my excitement but was unable to suppress my beaming smile. I walked towards him and attempted to shake his hand, but he laughed and pulled me to him instead.

"You didn't think that I fell for that interview guise, did you Ann?" he whispered as he held me. "I knew you would be beautiful."

I guess he feels the same way I do.

In his arms, I said nothing but hugged him back and was unable to stop smiling. The chemistry was incomparable to anything I had before experienced. Our connection was sealed; there was no going back now. After that, we were inseparable. The physical and emotional chemistry was there, there was no doubting that, but there was something else between us. It was a deeper spiritual connection, and it was something that neither of us had experienced before. We did sometimes fight—loudly. After an argument, we would both freeze the other person out for a couple of days, then come back together, agreeing to disagree about the topic, and turn our love for one another right back on—no grudges held. I stayed in Brazil for six months, working with the people of São Paulo, side by side with Armond, and continuing to write freelance for the *Washington Post.* By then, we both knew that we were meant for each other. We had become each other's best friend. Finally, though, I had to return home after using up most of my savings.

We arrived at the airport late, and I missed my flight. When the attendant told us the plane had just departed, Armond and I just looked at each other. No doubt it was accidentally on purpose. Thankfully, the airline was nice enough to re-book me two days later. That only drew out the pain we felt about leaving one another.

During my flight back to America, I cried bitter, inconsolable tears. Armond's work was in Brazil, and my work was in the USA.

When my plane landed, I had a voicemail waiting for me. I sat down on the unmoving luggage conveyor to listen to the message.

"I know you won't get this until you land, which means that you probably had an awful flight. I'm sorry about that. I want you to know that I love you, Ann, and I've given notice that I'm resigning. I'll leave Brazil in three weeks…to be with you…if you'll have me," he said humbly. "Call me," he said at the end, sounding excited.

Elation flooded me; I was so grateful. Tears of joy exploded from my eyes as I stood. Other passengers stared; I didn't care.

Armond proposed to me the day he arrived at Dulles Airport. Years later, we would talk about our parting in Brazil, and both of us recalled how we felt like being halved, torn in two that day. Neither of us could deny our uncommon connection.

After he proposed, we began to plan our simple wedding. The hardest detail was my dress—I wanted to make it myself. Once I'd finally finished that, the other details were easy. The ceremony would be at the home of some of our close friends. Another friend who played the guitar would be in charge of the music.

I remembered the day vividly. I came out of the bedroom in my white renaissance wedding gown, holding a simple bouquet of white roses and baby's breath. As I rounded the corner into the living room, I met Armond's eyes, and he flashed his gorgeous smile. He came toward me, taking my hands in his and leading me to where the rest of our friends stood. I'll never forget the poem I wrote to him—and the vows I promised—the last stanza burned into my mind.

I pledge my loyalty—strong and true.
I will love you well, my dearest friend.

We were married at sunset in 1997; I was twenty-six years old. As we drove from our friend's house to our home, we drove up a ridge heading east. Above us, a full moon appeared, enormous in the clear sky, shining bright orange. It seemed to us that we had a celestial blessing.

Our daughter was conceived on our wedding night. We decided to name her Elinor because it meant *bright and shining light that drives away ignorance and suffering.* We wanted her to bring compassion to the world. Elinor was such a beautiful baby, easy and joyful, and the three of us were a close family until Armond's death.

* * *

It always comes to that, I thought. I wish that I could just remember the perfection we had. Most people never get to have it. Most people settle. Most people give up. Armond and I were conscious of it. We lived in the moment, stacking up perfect days on top of perfect days.

I had stopped the potter's wheel and sat staring at the ceramic piece I had just created. It was beautiful—a bowl that he would have loved. I decided to fire it in Armond's favorite color, eggplant purple. As I took the wire and cut it off the wheel, I moved the piece onto the drying shelf.

I'd take it to the kiln on campus and have it fired.

Later, as I lay in bed, exhaustion snuck in—a warm, welcome guest. Sleep came quickly.

CHAPTER 12

BELLINGHAM, WASHINGTON
THE YEAR 1988

Just before graduating high school, I went down to the Bellingham Air Force recruitment center and took the entrance exam. I entered into the delayed enlistment program, so my active duty wouldn't start until after I graduated. My scores in the entrance exam designated me for an Air Force intelligence job, whatever that meant. It was a vague job description, but it looked promising for a seventeen-year-old.

I raised my hand and took the Armed Forces enlistment oath. Its words resonated in my mind:

I, Ann Torgeson, do solemnly swear (or affirm) that I will support and defend the Constitution of the United States against all enemies, foreign and domestic; that I will bear true faith and allegiance to the same; and that I will obey the orders of the President of the United States and the orders of the officers appointed over me, according to regulations and the Uniform Code of Military Justice. So help me God.

Six days after graduating from high school, I was flown to Lackland Air Force Base, Texas, for basic training. It was June and one of the hottest summers in history. As my enlisted group of Airmen traveled by bus from the commercial airport to the base, the sweat poured off me, my body shocked by the San Antonio humidity. Besides the heat, I didn't find basic training too difficult, except for the fact that I was taller than most of the women in my squadron, which gave the Air Force Training Instructors visibility of me that I would rather have opted out of. I quickly got used to hearing, "Torgeson! What's wrong with you?" screamed in my face by a giant with a Texas drawl. There was one occasion in basic training with my lead TI that I will never forget.

It was my squadron's day to learn to shoot M16 semi-automatic rifles; I was excited. We marched over to the shooting range and were given instructions and a demonstration by the TIs. My father and I had regularly practiced shooting pistols and shotguns starting when I was twelve years old, so I didn't expect to have any difficulty shooting the M16.

After the sergeant finished his instructions, the lead TI gave us one last warning: "Do not…I repeat…*do not* even consider shooting any of your fellow Airmen. Gonzalez—don't even *think* of pointing that weapon at any of your compatriots from Harlem. Is that understood?" the Texas TI bellowed.

"Yes, *sir*," we responded in unison.

Gonzalez wants to shoot someone? I was grateful to have heard Gonzalez affirm the TI's instructions.

The senior TI reluctantly gave us our M16s, with an evil look towards Gonzalez. The junior TI, Sergeant Pick, worked with us hands on while we loaded our weapons. Then we practiced. Once the TIs were confident that we wouldn't shoot each other, they moved on to describe our target practice. We would be shooting at the target fifty feet away. Sergeant Pick gave us the go ahead, and we started to shoot.

No big deal, I thought as I began to fire.

I calmly unloaded my magazine into the target with practiced hyperfocus. Before I knew what was happening, I was yanked up by the back of my collar, and my weapon was seized by the Texas Terror while he screamed his now familiar line.

"Torgeson! What's wrong with you?" he raged, a few inches from my face.

"Nothing, sir," I replied, dumbfounded at what could have enraged him.

"Why did you fire all your rounds?" he stormed. The expression on his face started to scare me a bit.

"Sir, I thought that's what we were instructed to do," I timidly replied.

"Stand over there at attention," he snapped, pointing to the wall behind us. "And if you move one little muscle, you'll find yourself repeating basic training like all the other washouts."

"Yes, sir," I obediently replied, perplexed about my error.

I stood at attention as commanded, my back against the wall, facing the rest of my squadron. Sergeant Pick pushed the electric button, moving all the targets forward to assess the squadron's shooting accuracy.

As the targets came closer, Texas Terror hollered, "Well I'll be a son of a gun. We've got a sharpshooter," he hollered, staring at one target.

I could see that everyone else had fired one bullet, while I had unloaded my entire magazine. *So that's why he's angry.* But the target the Texas Terror held was mine. My bullets had all penetrated either the bull's eye or the ring next to it. Suddenly, I felt a bit smug.

Then I heard, "Torgeson, get over here, pronto."

I stepped forward to the TI immediately, then resumed standing at attention.

"Torgeson, how did you do that?" he spoke in my face, with his rage now replaced with astonishment.

"Sir, my father taught me how to shoot when I was a young girl."

"Well ya don't shoot like a girl," he responded with a smirk, leaning into me.

I didn't smile. I was putting every ounce of energy into keeping an indifferent expression, but I wanted to laugh out loud with joy.

"Well, thanks to him, you'll stay in our squadron." He chuckled. "Maybe you should have joined the Marines—they could use some girls who can shoot. Now back up against that wall at parade rest," he commanded, simmering down from his hot boil.

Thanks, Dad.

I wrote my father a letter the first chance I got, telling my M16 story. I received his reply a little over a week later. He said simply, "Good job on that target practice, Airman." Dad was a Navy veteran and a man of few words about the military, but I knew he was proud of me.

After showing my skill with the M16s, both TIs treated me respectfully through the rest of basic training. My shooting reputation followed me to Keesler Air Force Base in Mississippi six weeks later, where I was to begin my formal training in Air Force Intelligence. I still wasn't sure exactly what that entailed. As I reported for duty after my flight, the sergeant who processed my incoming paperwork looked at my name and said, "You're not the M16 sharpshooter, are you?" I guess news traveled fast in the Air Force.

My first task at Keesler was to complete fourteen pages of forms, detailing all eighteen years of my life; it was nearly a page per year of my life. Apparently the Air Force was investigating my eligibility for a Top Secret/Special Intelligence security clearance. Until the security clearance was completed, I wasn't allowed to learn anything about my intelligence assignment. While I waited for my TS/SI security clearance, I attended forty hours per week of classes on and off base.

This formal training was in addition to the forty hours of basic training classes I had already taken at Lackland—on Air Force history, combat, and war strategy. At Keesler, I completed a number of psychological classes. The Air Force seemed to be intent on educating me about the paranormal, which was fascinating to me. I had no idea what I'd be doing with all that knowledge, but I figured that my job was going to include some crazy psychological scenarios.

After three months at Keesler, I was ordered to Langley, Virginia. That's when I learned that I was being assigned to the CIA.

CHAPTER 13
LANGLEY, VIRGINIA
THE YEAR 1988

I landed at Dulles International Airport and took the CIA shuttle to Langley. It dropped me at the Air Force in-processing station at the CIA, where I signed in. The next day, I reported for duty directly to my Commanding Officer. His assistant sent me into his office.

"Sir, Airman Torgeson reporting for duty," I reported in with a salute.

He returned my salute from his seat and then held out his hand for me to deposit my orders. I gave them to him, then moved to stand at attention, looking straight over his head to the wall behind him.

"At ease, Airman."

I moved to Parade Rest, tucking my hands behind me, and looked at him. He was a lean forty-something, with an angular face, black hair, and very small eyes.

"You're the sharpshooter," he exclaimed, looking at the papers.

"Yes, sir."

"And you're going into intelligence?" he asked, looking at me, more of a statement of fact than a question.

"Yes, sir."

"We could use you better in other places, you know. But the CIA's got our kahunas in a vice on this one. Apparently you tested pretty high on the CIA's tests at Keesler, and they're insisting upon getting you. I'd rather we use you as a sniper, but Congress won't allow us to put girls on the front line of combat."

What do I say to that? I thought, deciding that saying nothing was a good plan.

"What do ya think of that, Airman?"

Oh, crap.

"Sir, I'll serve wherever you want," I said, thinking on my feet.

"Right answer, Airman, right answer," he responded with a smile. "You could go far in the Air Force with that kind of answer."

"Yes, sir."

"Well, Airman, the CIA's gonna have to wait a while before they get you, 'cause your security clearance isn't in yet. Until then, I'm assigning you to the Nuclear War Special Duty Team. That's the closest you'll get to combat for now. My assistant will tell you where to report tomorrow. Welcome to the Air Force, Airman Torgeson," he said, standing.

I threw him a crisp salute, and he responded in kind. I turned sharply, leaving his office. Stopping by his assistant, she gave me a paper showing where I would report for duty the next day.

What the heck is the Nuclear War Special Duty Team? I thought as I strode down the hall, looking at the paper that the assistant had given me.

The next morning at seven o'clock, I reported for duty, then was sent over to the CIA for my polygraph, an essential element to obtain my security clearance.

I was intrigued about working at the CIA, especially since they seemed to want me so badly. I was patriotic and liked the thought that I could be useful. After having just turned eighteen years old, I hadn't had much time to get into any real trouble, but I was still scared that I would somehow fail the polygraph. I reported to the personnel department of the Agency and soon found myself in a little room, being hooked up to a dozen wires by a skinny guy in a black suit and a forgettable tie. Despite the tie, I was still intimidated, and I told myself not to freak out. The polygrapher had a personality as interesting as a cardboard cutout; he was so detached.

The polygraph seemed to be going along fine until about halfway through, when someone down the hall slammed a door.

Someone slammed a door, I thought in reflex.

At the same time as the door slam, the polygrapher asked me, "Are you secretly involved with foreign nationals?"

"No," I answered, but I could see that the machine's needles had registered my startled reaction to the slammed door, and the examiner wrote something on the output paper, appearing eager.

Cardboard man then began pummeling me with detailed questions about foreign nationals.

"Do you know anyone who lives in a communist country?"

"No."

"Do you know anyone who is plotting terrorism in the USA?"

"No."

"Do you know anyone who is involved in sabotage against the United States?"

"No."

"Have you ever met in secret with a foreign individual?"

"No."

"Have you ever seen classified information from a foreign national?"

"No."

"Have you ever been asked to provide classified information to a foreign national?"

"No."

The questions continued and then were repeated for sixty minutes. Instead of panicking, I became hyperfocused, as though my life depended upon the success of this polygraph. After two long hours, the examiner shut down the machine and finally asked me the question that he should have asked long before.

"What was going on when I first asked you the question about any involvement with foreign nationals?" he inquired intensely.

"Someone slammed a door down the hall," I explained. "I was startled."

"It's important during a polygraph that you focus on the questions and not exterior things," he exclaimed, exasperation seeping into his façade.

Right, I thought, *because I take polygraph tests all the time, and I should have known better.* I didn't respond out loud, but I watched as he unhooked me from the wires.

"We're all done here," cardboard man stated. "Your Commanding Officer will get the results after we analyze them and prepare a report," he stated, apparently dismissing me.

I could swear he isn't human.

"Thank you," I said as I turned to leave.

There was no reply from him. I overcame the temptation to slam the door on the bugger on my way out.

That sucked. I hope I never have another one, I thought as I escaped down the hall.

Four weeks later, I was called into my CO's office and told that my background investigation was complete, my polygraph results were in, and I was cleared to work at the CIA.

By that time, I felt that I was nearly an expert in reacting to a nuclear disaster. I'd worked and drilled with the nuclear team for weeks and was relieved to hear that I'd received my clearance and could be freed from the nuclear-obsessed crew. After all, there were only so many ways to read a Geiger counter.

I was scheduled to attend the CIA's newcomers briefing the following day. The class was for new CIA employees and all military personnel assigned to the Agency.

A female briefer outlined the Agency's history and its current organization, then went into an intensely serious explanation of the policies regarding sexual harassment and discrimination. She educated us about each level of security clearance and what each meant, and the whole class was drilled about the importance of gauging the need-to-know of co-workers or superiors. We also received an eye-opening tour of the vast agency facilities, which included the medical clinic, credit union, Ticketmaster, cafeterias, and the fitness center. The tour concluded when the guide took us past a row of at least twenty-five pay phones in sealed cubicles that were collectively called the phone bank. Stopping us, the guide instructed us not to use the phones except in a personal emergency. When I looked at the phone bank, nearly every seat was occupied.

So all the people who are talking in the phone booths right now are having personal emergencies?

I nearly broke out laughing but restrained myself. After the phone-restriction lecture ended, signaling the end of our tour and briefing, an Air Force lieutenant approached me and told me to follow him.

He took me into a room marked *Visitors*. From there, we entered a much smaller room. Lieutenant Smith—I'd seen the nametag on his uniform—closed the door, then handed me a large brown envelope.

"Read it," he commanded me.

Is Smith really your name? I wondered.

I felt like I held the secret of UFOs. I obeyed and opened the envelope. Inside the envelope contained one page with three lines of information:

Room: C4-336
Code: 99136
Report for duty immediately after indoctrination.

Thank goodness I know what indoctrination means.

After observing me open the envelope and read its contents, Smith opened the door and left without another word to me. I had no chance to ask him a single question.

Is this a test? How am I supposed to know where this room is? I thought, dumbfounded, staring at the door of the cubbyhole room.

Okay, let's break it down, Ann. What's C4? I coached myself.

I left the cubby room and approached the newcomers' briefing instructor, who was still in the hall, answering questions from my classmates.

"Excuse me," I asked during a lull in the questions. "Can I get a map of offices? I'm supposed to find a room but don't know my way around yet," I asked her.

"We don't have maps of CIA headquarters, but if you'll tell me the office number, I'll help direct you," she replied courteously.

"It's C4-336," I replied.

"Okay, the four means it's the fourth floor. The first number after that is the department—you're going to department three. The room number is thirty-six. Head over to the elevators. You'll need to show your badge to the guard there. Once you get up there, the departments will be numbered sequentially. If you see any doors without numbers, skip them," she patiently explained.

"Thank you," I sincerely replied.

What's the C stand for? I wondered but figured I'd better not ask.

Heading to the elevators, I was stopped by a guard who put his hand up, blocking my path.

Stopping, I looked up.

"I haven't seen you before," the six-foot-four black guard stated in a deep bass voice.

"Today is my first day," I replied with a forced smile, looking up at him. I raised my badge from the chain around my neck and held it next to my face—just like the newcomers' briefing instructor told us to.

"My name is Ed," he offered.

"I'm Ann...Ann Torgeson," I nervously responded.

"No need for last names, Ann. Nice to meet you; go on ahead," he vibrated.

Once in the elevator alone, I thought, *Welcome to the CIA.*

After reaching the fourth floor, I exited the elevator and turned left—that being the only choice—then turned left again. The floor was covered with square tiles from the 1970s and was obviously buffed regularly, though snags of dirt were collecting at the edges of the hall. There were neither art nor posters on the walls, which were all painted a light gray. It looked like a prison.

I scanned the room numbers…51…52…53…I was going the wrong way. I turned back the other way and saw the numbers starting with 01…02…03…

Finally I reached 36. I hoped this was where I was supposed to be. I opened the door. Ahead of me was another door with a cipher lock on the outside, containing a series of five vertical stainless steel buttons just below the silver door handle. Above me in the corner of the ceiling, tilting down, was a large camera. I sighed.

They're not kidding about this little test.

I removed the letter from the envelope once more and, hastily opening it, entered the code from the second line into the cipher lock, pushing in each button until they clicked. I'd never opened a cipher door before—clearly this was on-the-job training. I hoped I was doing it right. I didn't want to look stupid on my first day.

They're probably watching me right now, laughing their butts off, I thought as I tried to turn the doorknob and it refused to move.

Oh man, I thought. *I got the number wrong. Now I know they're laughing.* I felt my face flush.

I looked at the paper again and reentered the number, careful to push each button slowly until each clicked. I tried to turn the knob again. It didn't budge.

Oh, come on.

Then it occurred to me to push the door open, instead of trying to turn the knob.

Bingo. I smiled stupidly at the camera as the door swung open.

I hope that was a pass/fail test.

CHAPTER 14
LANGLEY, VIRGINIA
THE YEAR 1988

The cipher door swung heavily shut behind me, nearly catching my large black Air Force-issued handbag.

My elation from having successfully negotiated the cipher test quickly deflated when I realized that I stood in another long prison hall, with a series of doors marked with letters. I stood still.

Hmmm, I thought, *I wonder what's behind door A*?

Just as I was about to knock on it, a tall man of medium build emerged from another door farther down the San Quentin hallway. He approached me with a smile.

"Hello, Airman Torgeson. I'm Bob Hadley," he said pleasantly, extending his hand.

He appeared to be in his midforties, with kind brown eyes, a head full of gray hair, and a bit of a double chin that accompanied his extra fifty pounds. He had a presence of quiet authority.

"Hello," I responded, shaking the hand he offered me."Since you know my name, does that mean I'm in the right place?"

"Getting through the cipher lock showed you that you're in the right place," he clarified.

So he was watching.

"I direct the project you'll be a part of here."

I nodded, but hid my confusion. *My Air Force supervisor is a civilian?*

"I'm pleased to be here, sir."

"Instead of you calling me sir or Mr. Hadley, how about we keep this informal, and you call me Bob?" he asked, though it seemed more like instruction.

"Yes, sir. You can call me Ann, if that's not against any protocol."

"We're a pretty tight group here, Ann. You'll find that we don't get too wrapped up in formal protocol within our project. You can call all team members by their first names."

Cool.

I replied with a simple smile.

"Another thing. Because of the sensitivity of our work here, you fall under a special arrangement between the CIA and the Air Force. Starting tomorrow, when you report for duty here, you'll dress as a civilian. No Air Force uniform, nor anything that identifies you with the military. Wear your hair down, not up like Air Force regulations dictate. And don't bring that Air Force-issued purse on your shoulder," he cautioned.

Why is that? I wondered.

Answering my silent question, Bob said, "We don't want to call attention to any military personnel on this project. Foreign governments would like nothing better than to target one of our military personnel for espionage against us. You'll likely remember learning in basic training about the damage done by the Walkers?"

I nodded grimly.

John Walker was an officer of the U.S. Navy. His initial role in radio communications gave him access to highly classified military secrets. He quickly moved up the ranks as a communications officer. In time, though, Walker became disenchanted with the Navy, and in 1967 he committed his first act of espionage when he sold information about Navy ship movements to the Russian KGB, after walking in the front door of the Soviet embassy in Washington, D.C. to make contact with them.

Walker continued spying, passing thousands of classified documents to the Soviet Union while in the Navy. He involved his wife, Barbara, and then recruited his brother, Arthur, and his son, Michael. The Walker spy ring was active for eighteen years and was one of the most damaging acts of espionage ever committed by U.S. citizens. They aided the Soviets in deciphering more than a million classified naval messages. When asked how he had obtained so much top-secret information, Walker was quoted as saying, "K-Mart has better security than the Navy."

"In our program," Bob said, "we mask your military identity as a protective measure against you being targeted by an espionage recruiter. Foreign powers intentionally target our military because you make less money than civilians here. You don't fit the mold, Almost all military spies have been men—all of them older than you. The good news for you is that you can put aside your uniform for the next few years, except for any official Air Force business that your CO calls you in for—of course that's all outside the Agency."

"Got it," I said. "No uniform, military hair, or other stuff, starting tomorrow."

"Right. Now that we've got that out of the way, I want to hear about your sharpshooting," he inquired, smiling.

Again. News travels fast.

"My dad taught me when I was young," I offered as an explanation.

"It looks like our group will be in good hands, then," he said with a chuckle as we stood in the stark hallway.

"Sir…Bob, I mean…can you tell me what the group is?"

"We're part of the Science and Technology Division, which is one of four overall organizations in the CIA. Science and Technology researches and then develops methods and technology to improve intelligence gathering. Our organization creates all the cool 007 spy technology, like the poison pen that James Bond used."

I smiled, enjoying his reference.

"We roll into the Clandestine Service. Our organization develops technical programs to gather information from foreign sources. But instead of explaining our little project, let me show you."

We moved down the long hall and through a doorway, entering a very large room, at least one hundred feet wide and nearly as long. The room was furnished and lit so that it felt like a very comfortable and sizeable living room. Seating was scattered throughout, some of which was occupied. The colors in the room were predominantly soothing shades of green and blue. The room made me want to sit down and put my feet up.

"Welcome to Project Stargate," Bob offered, with his right hand extended, sweeping outward.

I smiled in reply.

"Let's go over to one of the training pairs and watch, then I'll explain after."

We sat down near a woman in her thirties and a man about ten years older. We were close enough to observe them without interfering. The woman had long blond curly hair, very fair skin, piercing hazel eyes, and an oval face. She was tall and thin, a natural beauty. She was deeply focused on what was in front of her; it was obvious that she was a trainee. Her instructor was Hispanic, of medium build and height, and quite ordinary looking. He kept working with the woman, paying us no attention.

In his hands were numbered envelopes. The woman selected the number four envelope, then sat back in the sofa with her clipboard, pen, and paper. She was clearly calming herself with her eyes closed for about a minute. She then opened her eyes, wrote down the date and time and TARGET 4. I noticed that the number corresponded to the number on the envelope she had chosen. After a short while, she began to sketch lines and shapes. She also wrote down sensory information—some colors, textures, and tastes. It was like watching someone observe something that I could not see; it was intriguing. After about ten minutes, she wrote END at the bottom of her paper, along with the current time. She then removed her paper from the clipboard and handed it and the unopened envelope to her instructor.

The man then put the paper on the table and opened the envelope to reveal its contents. He displayed three distinct pictures: a skyscraper in the sun, a red apple, and a man with a cowboy hat. Clearly, the woman had sketched the skyscraper and the cowboy hat, and she had written down "sweet," which must have referred to the taste of the apple.

Are they doing ESP experiments here? I wondered.

Bob stood up silently, nodding his head to the instructor and the woman, and led me away from the pair gently by my elbow. We entered a glass observation room where we could watch the pair training. Once the door was shut, he began to explain.

"You probably think it's a type of ESP experiment, right?"

Looking sheepish, I nodded.

"Well you're going down the right road—but what we're doing here is called *remote viewing*. In remote viewing, we do use extrasensory perception, but we also use specific protocols, so our technique and environment is controlled, and the technique is learnable. A trained remote viewer can sense an object, person, or event existing anywhere, *in any time*—present, past, or future. Time and space is not a limitation in remote viewing. What we're doing here is training individuals to remotely perceive intelligence targets of foreign entities."

Wow. My mind was reeling.

"Now you can understand why you were not allowed to know anything about our project before you were granted a TS-SI clearance."

"Yeah, I understand," I confirmed, nodding seriously.

"Ann, the work we're doing here uses a kind of parapsychological intelligence." Bob paused and then asked, "Have you ever heard of astral projection?"

"You mean like Shirley MacLaine's out-of-body experiences?"

"Yes, *some* people—like MacLaine—call astral projection an out-of-body experience," he responded, seemingly irritated.

"The beginnings of remote viewing were discovered during astral projection research conducted at Stanford Research Institute in the seventies. The research we were funding at Stanford was very interesting. Let me explain the breakthrough we had there," he said, looking to me for understanding.

I nodded.

He continued, "We realized that geographical coordinates were ultimately necessary for precognitive remote viewing. This is similar to how memory works. When you remember what you did yesterday, you think about a location, and an image forms in your mind. The same principle is used here, only in reverse. If we needed to know about something before it happened, like an enemy plot, for example, then the targeted coordinates were essential to our success. We also learned that some viewers were naturally predisposed through their genetics to be very accurate remote viewers. We could only identify this genetic predisposition when it was manifested by the individual, in the form of vivid dreams, astral projection, extrasensory perception, mental telepathy, and other natural gifts. Once we knew of the necessity to use geographic coordinates and to select gifted viewers, we began Project Stargate here at the CIA."

"So the Stargate program uses all of those gifts?"

"Yes. We've learned a great deal so far. You'll learn more as you're trained."

"I look forward to it."

"You should know that other government and non-government organizations do not realize that Project Stargate is still live here. Those organizations believe that we passed this program on to other agencies. Ann, you'll be protecting this knowledge for the rest of your life, and you can never speak of it to anyone outside our group. Now you understand what I said earlier about family," he stated with seriousness, looking directly at me.

"I do," I responded, although I felt unnerved by his statement.

"You might want to know that we selected you for this project because of your score on the parapsychological tests you took at Keesler. Although, the Air Force tests at your recruitment center were our first indications that you could be an asset. A portion of that test reveals the natural gifts that we're seeking. We rarely add new personnel to our project. You are the first Air Force participant, and the youngest."

I was humbled by his words. "I'm eager to get started."

"Let me introduce you to our team members," he said, standing.

I also stood, facing him.

"John O'Brien, who I'll be handing you off to in a minute, will be your training partner. You'll work with him every day. He's eccentric, but I think you'll be able to overlook some of his odd tendencies."

What tendencies? I thought nervously.

"My door is always open. You can speak to me about anything at all. Don't forget that."

"Thank you for choosing me," I replied graciously with a smile.

"Let's go meet John," Bob said, leading me out into the viewing room.

As we crossed the room and approached the far side, a tall man with jet-black hair and broad shoulders strode around the corner, nearly running into Bob.

"Gabh mo leiscéal!" he cried out in an Irish brogue.

Unguardedly, I let a laugh escape my lips. The man had said, "Excuse me," but he seemed only slightly sorry.

"Oh come on, speak English, John!" Bob chastised.

"Gabh mo leiscéal! Tá brón orm!" John said, offering his apology. Then he looked over at me. "Now will you be introducing me to the young lass, Bob, or will you keep her to yourself?" he asked, meeting my eyes.

"Oh, brother. Ann Torgeson, meet John O'Brien, your trainer."

I held out my hand and offered, "It's nice to meet you," looking up to the thirty-something with a smile.

"And you," John replied, meeting my eyes while shaking my hand.

"He's harmless, Ann," Bob clarified. Then he pointed to John, saying, "You—behave yourself." Then Bob left us.

Nice introduction.

John looked at me, silent.

I dove in. "I only vaguely understood what you said, but I do recognize it as Gaelic," I said to him, trying to break the ice.

He lifted his dark brow in reply. "Now how is that, lass, with a name like Torgeson? There's no Irish in that name."

"It's my grandfather. His surname was Dunseath. His mother taught him the Gaelic. When I was a little girl, he would speak it to me. I never did learn much that stuck, but I can sometimes identify it as Gaelic when I hear it," I told him.

"Well then, maybe I can be your trainer in the Gaelic too—besides remote viewing," he said with a twinkle in his eye.

"Oh, I don't know about that. It's pretty hard for me," I cautioned.

"Maybe we can call your Irish blood to assist you—or maybe the wee fairies," he offered with a smile.

I laughed out loud.

"Why is it that you don't have much of an Irish accent except when you're speaking Gaelic?" I asked boldly.

He shrugged with brows raised, then smiled.

I smiled in return. I could tell that we were going to get on just fine, even though he was a bit odd.

"I went to university here, in America. I guess these blokes thought they needed a gifted Irishman to round out the CIA." He spoke in perfect English without an accent. "How would you like to meet the rest of the team?" John asked.

"Sounds great."

John then introduced me to the remote-viewing team, which numbered nearly fifty. We then returned to the observation room, which I learned was soundproof, and John began to explain more about the process of remote viewing.

"You observed Grace during her training, right?"

"Yes."

"What you didn't know about her viewing is how the photos were selected. They were chosen because they were strong images—not too complex, but capable of holding the viewer's subconscious mind. The three images were also distinctly different, which helps the trainer to tell the sketches apart," he said, looking to me for acknowledgement.

"How long has Grace been training?" I asked curiously.

"Nearly three months now."

"Wow," I blurted out, surprised.

"Does that seem like a long time to you?" John asked.

"No, the opposite. That doesn't seem like a long time to learn a new skill that you've never used before."

"Well, not exactly. We believe that the skill of remote viewing uses the same part of the brain used when dreaming. We think that's the limbic region of the brain—the part of your brain that controls emotion—but that hasn't been confirmed by scientists outside the CIA," he clarified. "So it just may be that remote viewing uses the same brain processes as when you dream."

I nodded, considering the implications.

John had been looking out the glass window into the observation room as he was explaining to me, but when he finished, he looked directly at me. It was as though he expected me to say something.

"I've had crazy dreams as far back as I can remember," I said softly.

"We know. The Air Force paranormal tests you took in Mississippi confirmed that. Most of the people we bring into this project are powerful dreamers. We're seeking that out in candidates, among other natural talents."

"Well at least someone will have the benefit of my dreams," I told him.

"Why do you say that?" John pursued.

"I dream things that I'd never consider imagining when I'm awake. Some of those things are hard to deal with sometimes," I confessed. I immediately became embarrassed about telling him this, and I could feel my face flush.

"You're not the first dreamer to feel that way. With time, you'll find its benefit to you in our work here," he said compassionately.

"Hmmm," I responded, still embarrassed.

"Since we're talking about dreaming anyway, let's talk about color. What's your impression of color in the viewing room ahead of us?" he asked me, intentionally changing the subject.

"Well, it's pleasant and has soothing color combinations."

"We've learned that dreams seem to be stimulated by the brain's limbic system—as I told you before. This system associates emotion with visual stimuli, including color. We also know that our autonomic nervous system unconsciously responds to color—"

"I'm sorry to interrupt, but what's an automatic nervous system?"

"It's *autonomic* nervous system," he corrected me.

I continued blushing.

"The *autonomic* nervous system controls the organs of your body—it's the automatic pilot part that runs your heart, stomach, intestines, and muscles—"

"Oh—I get it now," I interrupted.

"You are unaware of your autonomic nervous system because it functions in an involuntary, reflexive manner. For example, we don't realize when our blood vessels change size."

I nodded.

"The autonomic nervous system responds to color. The color blue, for example, elicits serenity, inspiration, and communication. Green brings balance and calmness."

"It sounds very metaphysical—very Shirley MacLaine."

"Ann, don't say that name around Bob," he warned.

I swallowed nervously. *Too late.*

"I'm pretty sure he hates Shirley MacLaine," John added. John laughed as he observed my reaction. "You already said that to him, didn't you?"

"Uh-huh."

He laughed harder.

"Well, at least I'm giving you a good laugh," I said, slightly annoyed.

"No worries, lass. He already knows you're young."

"Well, now I know not to say it again."

"We all learn that way."

"You were telling me about how our bodies relate to color," I offered, trying to deflect the topic away from me.

"I was. Here's a little tidbit for you. The people who study time travel here believe that green governs it," John said.

"Are we time traveling here too?" I said excitedly.

"No—not yet," he chuckled in response. "That's another project. With our project, we've tried to think multi-dimensionally to open all possible channels for success in remote viewing. Project Stargate is all about outside-the-box thinking, and we've sought out others like you, who naturally possess that way of processing information."

"How do you know how my brain handles information?"

"The tests you took at Keesler tested your paranormal skills. Didn't you wonder what they were for?"

"Yes," I said, developing a thicker skin as our conversation continued. "So you're using color in the room to tap into the brain's limbic system?"

"Yes, exactly," John confirmed. "You're smart for a young lass," he remarked in his Irish lilt.

I smiled big. *He doesn't think I'm stupid. That's a plus.*

"So I've learned that you're looking for vivid dreamers and unconventional thinkers. What other qualities do you seek?"

"Intuition. Taking intuitive risks is essential for success in remote viewing. You have to trust impressions that you're not sure of. Sometimes information will not make sense, so you'll have to intuitively trust what's right. Intuition is an important quality we need here. An individual either has it or doesn't. Yours is very strong. Most candidates are rejected after our psychological testing."

"Why?"

"For example, we might have a candidate who's a vivid dreamer and creative thinker, but we learn through our testing that he or she has some undesirable tendencies, such as grandiosity or a lack of remorse—sociopathic leanings. Or maybe they're emotionally weak. We require very unique talents in our project, but the person must be able to obtain a security clearance and be ultimately trustworthy. That makes you, Ann, quite unique, and we are glad to have you," he sincerely offered.

I'm glad to be here too…and glad I'm not a sociopath.

"Let's cover some more remote-viewing basics, okay?"

"Okay."

"The impressions you'll get when viewing will be competing with all the background noise that constantly occupies your mind. It's challenging to tune out these distractions, and you'll have to work to refine that skill. We've learned that images that are clear, bright, and sharp are noise—it's the opposite of what you would think. The mental images that we're seeking in remote viewing are indistinct or vague—something that seems *just out of reach.* It's similar to trying to remember the details of a dream just after you've woken up. As you practice, you'll work through the differences of what is the target data and what is noise."

"How do I learn the difference?"

"This is where sketching comes in. By sketching images you perceive, you'll hone your viewing skills. With time and practice, you'll find that your images start to take shape, accurately depicting your target. You'll also start to acquire other senses, like tastes, smells, and colors."

"Does it matter that I'm horrible at drawing?"

"No. It's not like you're drawing a scene to hang on your wall. Think of it as giving clues to a scene."

"Okay. How long will my training take?"

"It depends. Every remote viewer in training has had different growth rates. It could be years. We don't know. There doesn't seem to be a standard here. It depends entirely upon the individual viewer."

Years?

"It sounds like I'll spend my whole Air Force enlistment here."

"You will. Once we get you here, we won't let you go."

"Okay. When will I start my training?"

"Tomorrow."

Cool.

"Since your psychological testing told us that you're most creative in the early evening, your shift here will be three p.m. to midnight," he informed me.

I grinned. "Wow, you guys didn't miss anything. I certainly am a night person."

"Getting the details right is what we do here."

"Okay," I replied sheepishly.

"Why don't you split, and we'll start fresh tomorrow?"

"Okay."

"Don't forget—you can only discuss the project *here*, among our team. No one outside this room has any need to know what we're doing on this project. Even the name of our project is classified," he reminded me.

"Why is the project *name* classified?"

"All classified projects have a classified name—call it CIA tradition."

"Tradition…okay, got it," I confirmed. "I'll see ya tomorrow," I offered with a smile.

"See you then," he replied.

Holy cow, I'm in the big leagues now, I thought, returning down the hall I had come through earlier.

What will Dad think of this? I wondered, and then I realized that I couldn't tell him.

Continuing down the hall, I passed the alphabet doors and then came to the cipher door exit. Since I didn't have to enter a code to leave, I pushed open the heavy door and felt it quickly latch closed behind me. I breezed down the hall.

* * *

The following day, I easily aced the cipher-lock challenge.

As I entered the long hall, John met me there, his hand outstretched. "Hi, Ann," he swiftly greeted me. "From now on when you come to work, you can enter the viewing room through this door," he said, gesturing to the door we walked through, which was marked E.

"How was it when you left here yesterday, thinking through everything you learned?"

"It was incredible. I feel honored to be here. What you said about the connection between dreams and remote viewing pretty much blew my mind."

"Why is that?"

"Because dreams have been the nemesis of my life."

"Isn't it true that everything has its opposite, in order to balance life?" he asked me.

"I suppose so. I guess it could be that the opposite of nightmares is that I'll be able to see things in other times and other locations. I suppose it's the yin-yang balance my dad taught me about."

"Exactly. Your dad seems like a smart man. Won't it feel good to be able to take that nemesis and use it as a blessing for your country?" he passionately asked.

I paused thoughtfully. "Yeah, it will."

"Are you ready to get started with your first lesson, then?" John asked with a smile.

"I am," I replied.

"You saw one of the beginning lessons yesterday with Bob."

"Yeah. Then Bob explained some basics to me in the observation room," I clarified.

"What do you say we jump in and try it, instead of just talking?" he asked.

"That sounds perfect."

CHAPTER 15

BELLINGHAM, WASHINGTON THE YEAR 2015

I was in my BYD, heading to the office the day after the Shanghai earthquake, driving with a half-conscious mind. Finally I pulled into an electric-only designated parking spot near the front door of AlterHydro. Lulu and I entered the 1910, making our way through the large vestibule where the office manager sat at the front desk, sulking into her keyboard.

"Good morning," I smiled cheerfully.

"Morning," she glumly responded, head down.

Maybe she's depressed.

Passing her, I rounded the corner and approached the stairwell. Raymond Brown saw me first.

"Ann," he called out.

I stopped. "Hey, Raymond. How are you? I haven't seen you much lately."

Raymond and I had been friends since his first week at AlterHydro. He was one of the most attractive black men I had ever known, both on the outside and the inside. Raymond had the most joyous smile I'd ever seen, was six feet tall, and had the body of a professional baseball player, but he actually loved basketball. He was one of the kindest people I knew.

Raymond was the marketing director, and he was perfect for the job because he really did love people. We often had overlapping projects. He could get along with anyone and do it with a smile. In many ways, I looked up to him and respected him.

He was devoted to his family, but his wife was a jealous beast. One summer, AlterHydro hosted a summer picnic for everyone and their families, and of course both Raymond and I were there. He brought his wife and children; it was the first time I had met them. Any time Raymond and I spoke to one another, his wife would pop up out of nowhere, grab Raymond's arm, and hold tight, staking her claim. What was really irritating was that there was never an ounce of physical attraction between Raymond and me. I liked him as a person—and believed it was reciprocated—but there was never any reason for his wife to act like she did around me. She quite obviously felt threatened, and based on what Raymond told me, it wasn't just with me. The woman had rage too near the surface, and I wondered if one day she'd pull a Bobbitt on him. I steered clear of her whenever I saw her.

"I was visiting my family in Arkansas. I brought the boys and my wife."

"Oh, that's nice. I bet you had a nice time. Did you fly or drive?"

"We flew. I know, I know—two boys under the age of four—but I didn't have the vacation time to drive. My wife was so happy when we landed."

"I bet. I'm sure it was good to see your mom after so long."

"It was, it was. How's Elinor?" he asked, smiling.

"As you know, she's away, in her first year at the university. She's barely called me. But I guess I should be grateful that she calls me at all—even though it's only when she needs more money deposited into her account. Thank goodness she did one year of college through the Running Start program at high school. That saved a year of tuition."

"I did Running Start, too, and was able to finish my associate degree before I started at Western," Raymond said proudly.

"That's wonderful. Isn't it a great program?"

"It is that, it is that."

Raymond had the funniest way of repeating things. It always made me smile.

"So tell me how your boys are. Did Shawn's arm heal? Is he out of the cast?"

"Yes, thank you for asking. He's all healed and tearing around the house like a madman again."

"Oh, I'm so glad," I said, smiling.

"I can see that Lulu is doing well," he said, reaching down to pet her.

"She is. She's still running alongside me on the treadmill," I boasted.

"Lulu's the only dog I ever knew who did that."

"If I didn't have her running with me, I think she'd be tearing up our headquarters." I laughed.

"I could see that, I really could."

"Well Raymond, duty calls me to the dungeon, so I've gotta run."

"It was good to see you. Let's catch up sooner rather than later, okay?" he asked.

"That sounds good—lunch," I offered.

"Mexican," he replied.

"Next week," I clarified.

"Okay, done." He smiled. "See you then, Ann. Good to see you."

"Good to see you, too," I confirmed with a wave. Lulu and I started making our way down the stairwell.

As the blast of cool, damp air came up my nostrils, I saw my co-workers already in.

"Hi, guys," I greeted loudly with a wave.

"Hi, Ann," they responded in unison and then looked at one another across the room.

I laughed.

"Edwin, what's on the microwave menu today?" I stopped, bantering.

"I never know that until I get further into my day," Edwin replied seriously.

Paul and I both laughed out loud.

As I moved to my desk, Paul left his computers and came over to me. I started unpacking my workbag as Lulu took her rightful place on her dog bed.

"Can you believe that earthquake?" he asked me.

"I can't. It freaked me out," I responded, meeting his eyes.

"Did you know someone there?"

"Well, not exactly," I hesitantly responded.

There was silence between us, and he looked at me with questioning eyes.

"It looks like I should pull up a seat."

"You know, can I take a rain check and maybe talk with you at lunchtime? Do you want to run outside today, with Lulu?"

"That sounds great, and it's supposed to be a beautiful afternoon," he confirmed, obviously pleased with my invitation.

"How about we head out at twelve thirty?" I suggested.

"Okay. Twelve thirty it is. I'll meet you just outside the foyer," Paul agreed.

At twelve fifteen, Lulu and I went to the gym locker room to change.

"Lulu, it's a special day. We're running outside today."

Her bottom wagged. *Does she know what I'm saying?*

I took Lulu's leash, and we headed toward the foyer, past the glum office manager. We met Paul outside as planned.

He ran on the street side; he had an old-fashioned sense of chivalry about him. I ran next to him with Lulu on my left. She did love to run. We had gone about two miles, chitchatting the whole time.

"So tell me what's up," he prodded.

He sure is direct, I thought, glancing his way. It unnerved me a bit, being this open with Paul. I had not confided in a man since Armond's death.

"It was the strangest thing," I started slowly in breathless jog-talk, and then I decided to dive right in. "This morning, I awoke from a vivid dream. I'd traveled to Shanghai. It was so real that I didn't even realize it was a dream right away. I remember every part of the dream, too—every taste, scent, color, texture, feeling, symbolism, and even the cultural significances. At the end of the dream, there was an earthquake starting in the hotel I was in. That's when I woke up. It took me a few seconds to realize that I was home and not in Shanghai. Once I realized that, I knew something was really wrong. I asked my computer for the news, and as she began, I was horrified to learn of an earthquake there," I said loudly, speaking above the sound of cars as we ran up to the entrance of Boulevard Park.

"It sounds like a coincidence."

"I don't think so—"

"Why?" he interrupted.

How much can I tell him? I wondered.

"There's more, isn't there?" he said, interrupting my thoughts and surprising me.

"You might find it a little crazy—"

"I like a little bit of crazy," he reassured me, glancing my way with a smile.

"Okay, here goes nothing—"

He put his arm on mine to slowly stop our running. We both immediately touched our pace watches to hold the time.

"Ann, you can trust me," he said ardently, looking straight into my eyes.

I tried to maintain eye contact, but there was such intensity in them that I had to look away. I looked out at the sailboats in the water instead.

He laughed.

I didn't say anything.

"I know trust is hard for you," he said. "I don't know why, but I can see that it is. I want you to know that I know a thing or two about loyalty, and you have mine. You just don't realize it yet."

He stood closer, both of us still breathless from the jog.

"Tell me what it is about the dream that's got you spooked."

I started walking along the wooden boardwalk that followed the shore, and Paul followed along.

"In the dream, I found something," I started.

"What?"

"A Herkimer diamond."

"You mean a quartz crystal?"

"Yes."

"Okay, you found a Herkimer crystal. Did it mean something to you?"

"Well…I found it in my bed with me when I woke up," I said quietly.

"What?"

"In the dream, I found this Herkimer diamond that my father and I discovered when we were rock hounding in New York when I was a young girl. I lost it many years ago. I found the crystal in the dream, and when I woke up, it was right there," I blurted out, looking over at him.

"So you found a crystal like the one from when you were a kid. Do you have other quartz around the house?" he asked, trying to explain it.

"The crystal in my dream was the *very one* I found with my dad. It's extremely rare and identifiable. When I woke up, it was there…with me," I repeated with exasperation.

I could see that he finally understood, because his eyebrows rose, his eyes got big, and he was silent as we walked along the path.

"That's weird," he exclaimed.

Now that I had his attention, I dove right in. "This particular crystal awakens a spiritual connection to God, so that the wearer can seek their higher purpose. It's very special. My dad told me that it allows for energy to flow in both directions, because it's double terminated."

"I know a little bit about quartz. It consists of one part silicon dioxide and two parts oxygen. It's the most abundant mineral found on the earth's surface," he said, slightly lecturing.

"Now how do you know that—right off the top of your head?"

Smiling, he replied, "Oh, I rock hounded too, when I was in college."

"You're just full of surprises."

"I've been a geek for a *long* time."

I laughed. He was a funny guy.

"What do you know about quartz crystals?" I asked.

"They vibrate when they're exposed to electricity—they actually expand and contract, creating the vibration."

"Just like a living thing," I commented, as we neared the end of the boardwalk.

"Interesting, huh? Quartz can actually generate an electrical field."

I nodded.

"It's called piezoelectricity. When a quartz crystal is cut into a specific shape, and then voltage is applied to an electrode near the crystal, electricity is generated. When the voltage is removed, the crystal creates an electric field during its return to its previous shape. So a crystal can actually work like a circuit does. Oh, I gotta tell you about something when I was nine years old and a Boy Scout—"

"No way—a Boy Scout?" I interrupted, my mouth hanging open.

"It's true. I got this diagram of how to make my own crystal radio from my dad's *Popular Mechanics* magazine." He seemed to transform into his boy-self. "I took a quartz crystal, attached it to a brass cup, and then touched a wire to various points on the crystal, finding the signal. The radio was fully powered by the crystal, through piezoelectricity. This was the first true wireless technology, but without batteries," he stated, proud to relay the story.

"I had no idea," I said, amused by him.

"Quartz crystals are used to make electronic sensors, although those crystals are now made in laboratories. Billions of crystals are manufactured in labs every year, to be used in computers, cell phones, and other stuff. You probably already know from history that they've been used in wristwatches and in radios since the 1920s. So the question of the day is, why would a crystal power generator morph from your dream into your reality?"

"I have no idea. Our Herkimers were phantoms."

"Wow, really? Those are very rare. I wonder if that increases their piezoelectricity."

"I don't know."

Paul nodded, obviously contemplating the possibilities. As we reached the end of the park and turned onto a street, leading us up into Fairhaven, I debated whether to explain the spiritual elements. He was a scientific guy, after all.

"You know, Ann," Paul said, "I can always tell when you have something you're holding back."

"Huh?"

"Like right now…you were gonna say something else, but then you stopped yourself, didn't you?"

"For a geek, you're pretty observant about people."

"Well, not all people. Just you," he flirted.

Okay, what the heck, I thought. "You're right. I was going to say something else. But first tell me, do you know anything about the chakras of the body?"

"You will be surprised to know, Ann, that I do yoga at home every morning."

"I simply don't believe you," I teased.

"I do. I know that there are seven chakras of the body and that they are energy centers. I also know that they each represent a different color. I have read that blockages can make you sick—or even twisted," he joked.

"You're proving to be the antithesis of every thought I had about geeks."

He laughed, as I hoped he would.

"So tell me about what crystals have to do with the chakras of the body."

"Okay. My dad said these double-terminated Herkimer diamonds would open the crown chakra, which he called 'The key to the soul.'"

"Wow, that's deep."

"Very funny. He said that our Herkimers could clear energy blockages of the chakras, and that you could know your higher purpose. So these Herkimers have spiritual significance."

"Ooh, it's starting to sound a little new age," he mocked.

I slapped him playfully on the arm but then moved my hand quickly, startled by the energy between us.

"My dad was a pretty spiritual guy."

"Was?"

"He died."

"I'm sorry, Ann."

"Well, thanks. It was five years ago. He dropped dead in his favorite plant nursery."

"You're kidding," he said astonished.

"Nope, right there in front of my mother."

"Oh man…"

"I think of it like this: he died in a place he loved, his favorite garden shop. He would have been happy to go that way."

"But in front of your mother?"

"Well, he probably would have said that it served her right. They had a volatile and complicated relationship."

"That's messed up."

"Yep, you're right about that. I sometimes wonder how I found true happiness in marriage, being raised in my dysfunctional family," I added with my guard down.

"Wait a minute—I thought you were divorced."

"Widowed, actually," I softly corrected him. "And that's something I'd rather not talk about."

"Fair enough. Tell me some more about your dream."

I told Paul the details of the dream. But I did not tell him about Armond's words to me as he died; that was just too intimate to reveal.

As we walked back toward AlterHydro, Paul stopped me again, touching my arm, and then turned to me.

"Ann…go out with me," he appealed.

"Okay," I replied without hesitation, excited by the chemistry between us.

"Wow, you're a difficult woman to convince," he responded sarcastically, clearly pleased.

"Do ya want me to take it back?"

"No. It's just—I've wanted to ask you for a very long time," he sincerely explained.

"Well, I'm not going to tell you the twenty reasons why I should say no. But I will be testing the loyalty you told me about. No one at AlterHydro can know."

"Fair enough. Test away. My loyalty is one of my biggest assets."

"Your biggest?" I joked irreverently.

He laughed.

"But you're gonna have to wait until I get back from Washington, D.C. Bennett has me speaking at a conference there."

"I'll wait," he said with a wink.

"Okay then," I smiled.

CHAPTER 16
BELLINGHAM, WASHINGTON
THE YEAR 2015

With Elinor due home for spring break this weekend, the last thing I wanted to think about or discuss with her was the Herkimer, especially considering Armond's last words before he died. After work, I went by the Co-Op to get some fresh ingredients for the weekend. I saw Summer restocking shelves.

"Is this what you've been promoted to, Summer?" I teased, surprising her while she leaned over a canned-goods shelf.

"A little bit of this, a little bit of that. That's why I'm here," she responded cheerfully, standing to give me a hug. "What're you up to?"

"Elinor is coming home this weekend for spring break."

"Oh, that's so nice. Is she bringing a boyfriend?"

"She'd better not. She's too young, and it's too soon," I replied.

"Yeah, yeah, yeah, that's what all moms say."

"I'm just happy she's coming home at all. She's barely called me since she went to college," I complained.

"She's a big girl now, Ann. She's all grown up."

"Well, not to me."

"Feed her well, give her some money, buy her some new clothes, and for goodness sake, Ann, don't ask her to do any chores while she's home," Summer said, schooling me.

"Who are you? WikiCoach?"

"I know it's tough without Armond, but let her go a little."

"You have the most uncanny ability to unnerve me at the most inopportune moments."

"That's a lot of big words. Be careful now. Don't hurt yourself."

I laughed at her sarcasm; her coaching wasn't lost on me.

"I know you'll have a great time while she's here."

"We will. I better check out. Enjoy your stocking," I offered with a wave.

As I went to the checkout, I pondered Summer's advice. She always knew what to say. Let her go, she'd said.

I'll try.

Lulu was the first to hear the rental car pull up in the driveway. I rushed to the door, seeking to embrace my daughter.

"Oh, hello there," I said, startled, as I met a tall, broad-shouldered man with olive skin, nearly black eyes, and very dark brown hair.

"Mom, this is Eliott Belle," Elinor said, holding his arm.

"Hi, Eliott. I'm sure you can guess who I am," I said, with a surprised smile.

"Hello, Mrs. Torgeson. I'm pleased to meet you," he offered sincerely with a beautiful smile, then bent forward and kissed me on both cheeks.

"French?" I asked him, as he stood on the porch.

"Très bon. My parents were born in France, but I was born here," he answered, as I watched his mouth. It naturally upturned at the corners, making him seem perpetually happy.

"Two points for you, Eliott. Elinor and I love France and the French," I pronounced with a smile. "Won't you come in?"

"Oui," he said, stepping into the house. Elinor stopped to give me a big hug while I stood beside the door.

"First of all, Eliott, please call me Ann. Second, it's been quite a while since I've been to France, so please don't judge my French too harshly," I cautioned him with a smile.

"Thank you, and I wouldn't think of it," he said politely in perfect English.

"Darling, where is the toilet?" Eliott asked Elinor.

"It's down the hall, to the left."

Eliott moved down the hall, and I heard the bathroom door close.

"Quickly, tell me why there is a six-foot Frenchman in my house?" I asked Elinor quietly.

"He's my boyfriend."

"I figured that part out. Why is he here, and why have I never heard of him until now?"

I remembered Summer and what she had told me in the store. *Had she known about Elinor's boyfriend?*

"I did mention that I had gone on a couple of dates, remember? Let's talk about this when we have more time," Elinor whispered.

"A couple of dates? But now he's here…okay, okay, we can talk about it later. I'm so glad to see you," I said, hugging her.

Elinor had thick brown hair and olive skin, courtesy of her dad's genes. From me, Elinor inherited a heart-shaped face, broad shoulders, and a rounded backside. She was a striking young woman.

Eliott returned from the bathroom and stood close to Elinor, with his arm around her waist. His smile matched hers, even though her mouth was smaller. I looked from Eliott to Elinor, and I could see that she was smitten by this dark, striking young man.

That night Eliott offered to get some cocoa from the store when we decided to make brownie pudding. Elinor and I finally had a chance to speak privately.

"The first thing I want to know is whether you told Summer about Eliott," I demanded good-naturedly.

"No, Mom. You're the first to know."

"Are you sure, because she said something to me about you bringing a boy home."

"She did?"

"Uh-huh."

"Maybe she's psychic," Elinor teased. "Mom, did you notice that both Eliott's and my names begin with E, just like Dad's and your names both start with an A?"

"Oh goodness gracious, Elinor. That's a silly little thing that Armond and I used to joke about. It has no significance."

"Mom, both you and Dad always told me that it's the unusual that you should pay attention to," she countered.

She had me there.

"How serious is it, Elinor?" I asked softly, looking into her eyes.

"He's the one, Mom," she replied, blinking evenly at me with her large hazel eyes and unusually long eyelashes.

"Why haven't you told me about him before now?"

"I know I should have. But I've just been so caught up with school—"

"And Eliott, I think," I interrupted.

"Honestly, I just wanted you to see him in person, instead of me describing him over the phone."

"You're so beautiful," I said, holding the right side of her face with my hand, unable to question her further. "Of course Eliott would love you. Who wouldn't? You're smart, beautiful, spiritual, and so insightful. Even from a young age, you were a mature old soul."

"I love you, Mom," she whispered, hugging me.

I hugged her back but refused to be distracted. "What else do you need to tell me?" I asked in her ear, sensing there was more.

"Be nice to him. Get to know him. Because he'll ask me soon, I think, and I'll say yes," she firmly stated.

"Okay, Elinor," I acquiesced, having learned long ago that to argue with her once her mind was set was futile.

"Promise me you'll have a long engagement—at least a year?" I pleaded.

"A year?" she blurted.

"A year," I repeated firmly. "You're only eighteen years old, Elinor."

"Nineteen in a month," she corrected.

"It's two months, Elinor, and if you wait until you're twenty, I'll send you anywhere you want for your honeymoon," I bartered.

"That's the groom's duty, mom."

"I don't care about those sorts of things."

"Well Eliott does," she said with a stern face.

"Tell me more about him."

"He's college poor, like me, but his family is well off," she said as we sat facing one another in the window seat overlooking the bay.

"How well off?"

"Well, his family is from Belle-Île; it's a French island off the Brittany coast, the west coast of France."

"And what, Eliott's family owns the Belle-Île island or something?" I joked, gesturing to the islands we could see through the window across Bellingham Bay.

"No. They own most of the chicken operations in Brittany," she replied, serious.

"Chicken farmers—that's what his family does? Please tell me they're organic chicken farmers, and not some kind of chicken factory."

"They're the most respected grower of chickens in France. Their operations are worth 1.5 billion Euros, Mom. When you order a chicken at the Ritz in Paris, you get a Belle," she proudly responded.

"Well then. I guess that'll do. Do Eliott's parents own the company? What's the name of it?"

"It's called Belle Poulet, and his father and uncle co-own it. His uncle lives there, in Brittany."

"So, is Eliott intending to continue in the family business after college?"

"He *is* planning to go into the family business, and as he told you, he's a double major: agribusiness and animal science."

"That's good. Let's recap. He's part heir to a billion-dollar corporation, smart, cute, and he loves my daughter. What's his spiritual condition?"

"Well, he's more practical than I am. But that balances me. He's what I'd call grounded spiritually," she proclaimed.

"Are you thinking of being married in Brittany? Will you move there once you graduate?" I desperately inquired.

"Settle down, Mom. We've decided to live in America, but Eliott will travel to Brittany regularly," she answered patiently.

"And the wedding? Where will that be?"

"Here, Mom, of course," she quietly assured me, meeting my eyes.

"I think I understand why you haven't been calling me now."

Elinor blushed. "I just couldn't tell you over the phone. I had to bring him."

"I can see that. Still…make it one year, when you're twenty. Agreed?"

"Fair enough. He won't like it, but he'll agree," she reluctantly gave her word.

"I'm sure his parents will be grateful."

We had a good visit that week, while I chatted with Elinor and became fond of Eliott. I could see how the two of them meshed, and I could certainly see the mutual affection they had for one another. He seemed like an honest, grounded young man, just like Elinor had said. It was sad when they left the following week, returning to the university.

"Well, Lulu, it's just you and me again," I said, petting her.

She whined, as though agreeing with me.

"How about you and I go for a run?" I asked. Her bottom began to wag excitedly.

CHAPTER 17
WASHINGTON, D.C.
THE YEAR 2015

Bennett was sending me to Washington, D.C. to speak at the annual conference for the Society for Technical Communication. I had no desire to lecture there, but when the Society asked me, Bennett got wind of it and pushed me ahead, thinking that AlterHydro would gain some free advertising through the exposure. The Society allowed me to choose my own topic, and I prepared a lecture called "Cut the Fat: How to Put Your Text-Bloated Documents on a Diet." At least it was catchy. I was happy to return back East, to visit with my friends, long-since missed.

I flew into Reagan National Airport in Arlington, Virginia, got a rental car, and drove into Washington, D.C. to the Dupont Hotel. It was just a few minutes from my favorite neighborhood, Adams Morgan, where I planned to visit friends during my stay. I pulled my rental car into valet parking at the hotel and was quickly assisted by the attendant. I'd never stayed in a Washington, D.C. hotel before, since I'd lived in D.C. and had no reason to. But the valet escorted me inside, with Lulu following close behind.

"Miss Torgeson is checking in," the valet told the front desk clerk.

"Good evening, Miss Torgeson," the short, stout clerk beamed. He was balding on top and had bulging eyes. *Homer Simpson's come to life.*

"Hello," I replied with a smile.

"I understand you're here to lecture at the Society for Technical Communication's annual conference. Is that right, Miss Torgeson?"

"Yes, I am," I confirmed. I hoped I was in a good room.

"We're pleased to have you." He punched some of the keys on the keyboard. His eyebrows shot up momentarily, and he looked back to me. "One of the conference sponsors has upgraded you to Level Nine here at the Dupont Hotel," he informed me, clearly impressed.

What's that?

"Have you stayed on Level Nine before, Miss Torgeson?"

"No, I haven't."

"Let me explain, then. Level Nine is intended for our special guests, you see. We will see to your every comfort through personalized service—" he began.

"I don't mean to interrupt, but I have Lulu, my dog, with me. She's fully trained. Is she going to be allowed on Level Nine?"

"Why of course," he exclaimed. "We aim to take care of every need that you have. We will even walk her for you," he told me cheerfully.

Is he on a happy drug?

"You're booked into one of our luxury suites on Level Nine, and Brian here will take you and...Lulu was it?"

"Yes, Lulu."

"Aha, very good. Brian will bring you and Lulu up to Level Nine and show you all the amenities."

"Thank you very much," I responded and began to turn. "Oh, excuse me…" I began, turning back to the desk clerk.

"Yes?" Homer replied. I felt the smile moving over my lips.

"Can you tell me which sponsor upgraded my room? I'd like to thank them."

He began to type something into the computer.

"I'm so sorry, Miss Torgeson. For some reason, there's no information in our system revealing who upgraded the room."

That's odd.

"Hmmm, okay. Thank you," I replied and turned to follow Brian.

Brian led the way up to Level Nine, talking the whole time about how great it was.

It's just a room.

When he opened the door to my suite, however, I started smoking the same stuff that Homer and Brian were. The corner room was covered on two entire sides with windows and had a view all the way to the Capitol Building and the National Mall. I stopped and gawked at the view. Brian stood near me, nodding his silent agreement.

"I lived in this area for many years and had no idea you could get this kind of view from Dupont Circle," I said.

"It's a nice view," he purred.

The room itself was appointed in leather and other natural textures. The bathroom was pure marble, with a Jacuzzi tub and a separate glass-enclosed shower. The room was luxuriously efficient. *I'm gonna enjoy that tub tonight*, I told myself.

As Brian explained the dedicated concierge on Level Nine, I started to zone him out, exhausted from my flight. Brian could see this, and he offered to have my room attendant unpack my luggage for me. I declined, instead opting for a bath. I gave him a tip, hoping twenty dollars was enough.

He glanced at it. *Clearly not offended—that's good.*

"Would you like anything else, Miss Torgeson? Perhaps we can walk Lulu for you?"

"I stopped at a park just before we arrived, so she's okay. But thank you, Brian."

"Have a good evening, then," he responded cheerfully, closing the door behind him.

Lulu had already found the dog bed they had put in the room, before I even noticed it. I sat next to her for a minute, rubbing behind her ears.

"So here we are, Lulu—back in D.C. Does it smell different?"

No answer.

"Thank goodness the airline allowed me to bring you with me in the passenger cabin."

Virgin Atlantic had broken new ground the previous year by issuing an advertising campaign with their new policy of flying not only humans but their pets as well. I'd never flown with Virgin's new policy, so I didn't know what to expect. They treated both of us perfectly, and she was allowed in the cabin right next to me, where a seat had been removed. In its place was one of Virgin's new dog-bed seats. It was a clever invention, which restrained Lulu with an adjustable harness so that she would be safe and not wander through the cabin. We were allowed to board first, with the other animal flyers, and a special pet attendant harnessed Lulu and explained that she had to remain restrained throughout the entire flight. The attendant discreetly explained that I could purchase a doggy diaper at any time. I giggled at that. She smiled. From my perspective, it was all worth the cost of a second seat.

Lulu snuggled into her bed, her eyes droopy.

I'd rarely ever seen her tired. "Lulu, I think you've got jet lag."

Elinor and I had picked out Lulu from a litter with four females. From the beginning, I could see that she was trainable with a joyful disposition. When she was a puppy, I trained her to ring a bell that I had hung from the front door whenever she wanted to go outside to potty. I found that her bell training was very helpful when we traveled.

I hung her bell on the hotel doorknob.

Turning on the water, I began to run my bath as I peeled off my clothes.

Being back in D.C. turned my mind back to my years with the CIA, as I soaked in the bath.

CHAPTER 18
LANGLEY, VIRGINIA
THE YEAR 1990

"It's been a year now, John," I pleaded with O'Brien.

"You think I don't know that?" he huffed. "How can a woman so young be so infuriating?" he fumed, glaring at me.

I remained silent.

"Ann, you think you're ready, and I think you need more training. We differ in opinion, and since I'm the elder—"

"Whoa, you better be careful there, John, her sensory IQ is much higher than yours," Bob cautioned, approaching us.

John shot Bob a nasty look for his interruption.

"She wants to go live. Not one viewer has gone live after only one year of training," John said, exasperated. "Grace has been training for longer, and she's not live," he passionately pleaded.

"Let's move into the observation room and talk about it," Bob commanded, nodding for me to join them.

John spun around and purposefully strode over to the glass room in front of us. When we were all inside, Bob closed the door behind him and turned to us.

"What were you thinking, having this argument in the middle of the viewing room?" he asked, looking from John to me and then back again, red in his cheeks.

"Lig dom! Fág dom i m'éinear!" John said, scornfully requesting that Bob leave him alone.

"Stop it, John. You're acting like an Irish baby!" Bob scolded.

"She's not ready, Bob," John stated with reluctant control.

"I am too," I said, defending myself.

"You," Bob said, pointing a finger at me, "be quiet for a minute, will you?"

I feigned zipping my lips closed.

"That's one of you. Now you." He pointed at John next. "Her sensory IQ is more than two hundred percent better than anyone we've ever had on our team, You've known that since we brought her here a year ago. You also know that her viewing success runs ninety-eight percent, John. Ninety-eight percent. The next most accurate viewer we've got, Grace, only achieves sixty-eight percent success. We haven't seen anyone like her since Joseph matched five out of six targets consistently back in the 1970s. And don't forget, Ann's the only viewer that has that one *special* thing in common with Joseph—she clinically died when she was twelve and had a near-death experience.

Silence hung in the air as we stared at one another.

"I think that we should use Ann while we have her. Don't forget that she's Air Force—we've only got two years or so left with her," Bob reasoned.

"We could compel her to stay for another two years past that, using the national security clause from the fine print when she enlisted," John offered, matter of fact.

Enlisted members of all the armed services agreed to be involuntarily extended for another two years past their four-year enlistment, should it be required for national security reasons. It was in the fine print of every enlistment document.

"What?" I questioned, irritated that John would even consider getting my enlistment extended another two years against my will.

"Ann, sit there and be quiet," Bob commanded me.

I tried to sit quietly.

"And you—don't bring up things that are nearly impossible to get approved. Do you know how high I'd have to go to get approval for an extension like that? The kind of visibility it would give our project is not something that I would ever want to happen," Bob grumbled.

"You could voluntarily reenlist, Ann," John pleaded very nicely.

I exploded. "Reenlist? Why don't you just make me live now, so we won't have to sit here and talk about me reenlisting when my four years are up?" I spat.

Bob looked to me and then John, annoyance on his face.

"John, you cannot compare her to Grace or anyone else here. I know it, so do you, and Ann certainly knows it. We've got a finite amount of time with her, and we cannot waste it training and training until we get it all perfect. As you know, there is no such thing as *perfect* in remote viewing."

Silence. Bob waited.

"Are you going to say something or just grow moss?" he asked John.

John faced me and calmly asked, "Do you think you're ready?"

"Yes, I do."

Turning to Bob, John reluctantly asked, "How do you want this to go?"

"First of all, can we all *sit down*? You two are giving me more gray hair," Bob said, sarcasm dripping from words that hung in the air.

We all sat facing one another as the heavy air began to vent out of the room.

"Ann, you said you're ready. Are you, truly?" Bob asked me directly.

"I am. I've felt it for months."

"I don't need to ask you why you feel that way, because I've been observing you."

I knew he'd been watching me on those monitors in his office. The viewing room was clearly wired for video, and those all fed directly into Bob's office and were recorded 24/7. Bob always explained it away, saying, "Our project is experimental, so we have to document activities."

"So she's ready. Let's go from there. You know the protocol, John. You've been here long enough."

"You want me to put her in the queue for assignments now?" John asked, a bit agitated.

"Yes. Let's throw her into the fire and see if she can breathe. Don't bother with the easy stuff. I want to see if her confidence is just an excess amount of pride or whether she's got the chops for this."

I felt like they were talking behind my back.

"We've got the target in Asia ready to go. Do you want to put her on that?" John asked.

"What level is it?" replied Bob.

"Level four," he somberly clarified.

"Sorry to interrupt, but how many levels are there, and what do the levels mean?" I asked.

"See? She doesn't even know what the levels are," John protested.

"Stop it. You're the one who trained her," Bob said in disgust. "Ann, there are five levels, with level five signifying that an enemy threat is imminent. The target John wants to put you on is level four, meaning that the threat is expected but not imminent. Are you up for that?"

"It's as good a time as any, so yes," I steadily confirmed.

"Start her on the Asian target tomorrow. We need her calm," Bob directed John, and then he stood to leave.

John nodded silently in agreement. I felt excited as John turned and looked at me.

"What?" I asked him, accusatory.

"Relax tonight, Ann. See you tomorrow afternoon," he said flatly and got up and left the viewing room, leaving me alone.

I rose, striding out towards the door of the viewing room.

I'm going live, I thought excitedly as I left the building.

The next afternoon, I was through the cipher lock like lightening. I couldn't wait to get started on my first live assignment.

In the viewing room, John handed me a piece of paper with map coordinates, minutes, and seconds typed on it. He knew nothing more about the target than I did—that way the session couldn't be influenced by him. There was no other information on the paper. On my lap sat a clipboard with a plain piece of paper, and I had a pencil in my hand. I studied the information on the paper that John had given me until I felt that I remembered it, and then I closed my eyes.

I started the Transcendental Meditation technique that the team had taught me over the past year. It allowed my mind to settle inward, past my own thoughts, to enter into pure awareness. My brain was alert but functioning with more subtle comprehension. I started my deep breathing exercises.

After twenty minutes in meditation, John delicately tapped my hand, which was our practiced indication that he would start asking me questions.

"What do you see?" he softly asked.

I opened my eyes and, staring at the clipboard, wrote the date and current time at the top, along with the word BEGIN, and then I began to sketch the images that were gently being revealed in the back of my mind.

As my drawing started to slow, John directed, "Describe your sensory impressions."

I continued sketching and began adding words to describe sounds, smells, and emotions.

Seeing that I was drawing a building of some kind, he gently prodded, "Draw the inside of the structure."

When I was finished, I wrote END, along with the current time.

John narrated, "It's a building with grounds laid out in detail."

"I think the building is underground. Maybe a basement?" I added.

"Eight individuals—"

"It could be that there are more in the background. That's how many there were in the main room with the big table," I interrupted.

John added notes to his own notebook from the information I just revealed.

"What's the fear?" he asked me, glancing at my words.

"The leader was the only one who felt no fear. But everyone else I could sense had fear. They've got firepower, John. I couldn't see what, but the fear the men carried was linked to whatever weapon they're intending to use."

"What are these words?" he asked, pointing to my paper.

"Code words."

"For what?"

"I don't know."

He made some additional notes in his book.

"You did well, Ann. It's enough to target them via satellite. We can also have the phones tapped for these code words," he said proudly. "I was wrong, Ann. You are ready. Why don't you go home, and we'll see what we can confirm by the time you come back in on Monday?" he offered.

"All right. Night, John."

"Goodnight, lass," he said affectionately with a smile.

As I left through the observation room, I noticed Grace sitting alone.

"They've got you live, I see," Grace said to me, seeming slightly jealous.

"Yeah, it felt like it was time," I gently replied.

"It's early, but anyone can see that you're special."

"Are you okay?" I asked, concerned.

"I'm fine. I've got a terrible headache, that's all."

"You had one the last time I saw you. Are you taking something for it?"

"Yep, just popped the pills. I just need to take a break for them to work before I head back in."

"Oh, okay."

"So was it what you expected?" she asked.

"Yeah, pretty much. It's not that different from training, really."

"Unless you get it all wrong," she replied.

I didn't know what to say.

"Don't mind me, Ann. It's this headache."

"Well, feel better, Grace," I softly offered, then turned to leave.

"Bye, Ann."

The next day, Bob told me what happened with the target that I viewed. Six individuals were apprehended, along with a cache of weapons in the basement of the old building. It was a successful remote viewing for the CIA, and I was able to help prevent a terrorist action. That felt good.

CHAPTER 19
WASHINGTON, D.C.
THE YEAR 2015

After my prep meeting with conference organizers was over, I planned to meet some of my old friends for dinner at the Red Sea restaurant in Adams Morgan. It was our old hangout, and it brought back fine memories of our group.

Running with Lulu to exhaust her never worked, but I tried. I left her in the hotel room while I went to dinner, asking the Level Nine concierge to check in on her once every hour till I returned.

Deciding to walk, since it would only take fifteen minutes, I left about a half hour early, just in case I was enticed to stop somewhere along the way. As I neared the restaurant, I could see it tucked in its familiar spot, framed in red. Since I had window browsed along the way, I arrived at the same time Jackie did. We had grown up together, and she had been my best friend for much of my life.

"Jackie, it's so good to see you," I said as I bent to hug her.

At five foot three, Jackie held herself taller than her height, never letting a thing get past her. She was smart and beautiful, with dark hair, fair skin, alert brown eyes, and a large, plump bosom on a petite frame that attracted men near and far.

"You look good, girl. The West looks good on you," she cheerfully observed.

I laughed.

"I've missed you," I responded.

She hugged me again.

"Let's get a table, huh?" she asked, moving toward the door. She was always the no-nonsense type.

Bathed in red from the outside in, the Red Sea restaurant was the epitome of exotic. The Ethiopian women who worked the tables each had their distinctive unique bone structure, perfect chocolate skin, and bright, lovely smiles. Along the walls were hung huge travel-bureau-style graphic posters of Ethiopia, which brought even more color to the large, open room that smelled like exotic spices. Ethiopian music piped throughout the restaurant in the background, but not so much so that it distracted from conversation.

Oh, I've missed it here, I thought nostalgically.

Jackie asked for a table for five near the front windows.

There wasn't one Ethiopian among all the restaurant patrons. Instead, the place was filled with Washington, D.C.'s food connoisseurs. It was a perfectly cheery place to come with friends.

"Let's just sit. The other three will be here soon anyway," Jackie suggested.

"That sounds good."

The waitress led us up the stairs to the front of the restaurant, overlooking the street.

"Will this be okay?" she asked us with her hand extended to the large round table.

"It's perfect. Thank you," I replied with a smile.

"My name is Alem. Just raise your hand when you are ready to order," she politely suggested.

Jackie and I sat next to one another, leaving space for three others opposite us.

"Why don't we order for everyone? We've done this enough times. We'll just order the sampler like always, plus a few extras," Jackie decided.

A smile erupted from my lips at the familiarity of it all.

Eating at the Red Sea was a communal experience. The food was served on a huge platter that resembled an extra-extra-large metal pizza plate. It was covered with a flat-dough bread called injera. Individual entrées were poured on top of the injera by the waitress as she named each dish. Patrons eat by taking their individual napkin-looking injera, tearing off a piece to grab meats, vegetables, and sauces, and then plopping the whole thing into their mouth for a taste extravaganza. It was here at the Red Sea that I first learned what steak tartare was. My friends thought it was a good idea for me to learn that it was raw spicy meat—by watching me eat a handful of it. I gagged and nearly hurled it all up while Armond, Jackie, and our other friends laughed. Once, when Armond and I were eating in Paris at La Fermette Marbeuf restaurant on the Champs-Elysees, I tried to trick Armond into ordering it, but he steered clear of my shenanigan. After the Red Sea incident, I loathed anything with the name *tartare*. Ethiopian food was dressed up with exotic spices, and as long as it was cooked, it was extraordinarily delicious.

"Along with the sampler, should we add the chicken doro wat?" Jackie asked.

Jackie called herself a vegetarian, but she ate chicken all the time. However, she never touched beef. It made no sense—but it was uniquely Jackie.

"Sure, sounds good. Let's also add the lamb lega tibs in the awaze sauce. I'm salivating remembering that," I added, looking at the menu.

"Everyone will love it. They'll already bring us a bunch of veggie dishes, so I think we've got it covered," concluded Jackie.

She raised her hand slightly so that Alem could see us to take our order.

After Alem left, we started to catch up, keeping an eye out for our three friends.

"So tell me how you've been," Jackie prodded.

"I've been good—very good. I feel like I've found a pretty good groove at AlterHydro. I like the work there. Plus, I get to bring Lulu to work."

"You do? I wish I could bring my dog to work with me," she said, pouting.

I laughed. Jackie was an artist and worked from her townhouse studio; she was allergic to dogs. Instead, she had what I called a cat farm.

"How many cats are you up to now?" I inquired, eyebrow raised.

"Well—four. Wait, wait, I know what you're about to say—" she preempted after seeing my mouth drop open.

"That's a lot of litter-doodle scooping," I interjected.

"No, no, you should see it, Ann. I got a little kitty door, straight out the back door. And I built a sand box for them—but I fill it with scoopable kitty litter."

"You're kidding. So you go outside and scoop the poop?"

"Yep," she proudly exclaimed.

"What do you do when it rains?"

"It's covered, like a little playhouse."

I laughed heartily. "Only you, Jackie, only you. Oh man it was gross when I roomed with you in your townhouse. I can't believe you left that nasty litter box in my bathroom. It was so gross when I went to take a shower with kitty litter stuck to the bottoms of my feet," I remembered, gagging a bit at the memory.

Jackie laughed hard and long at the memory. "Hey, you weren't paying rent. It was the price you had to pay, Ann."

"Maybe I *should* have paid you."

We both laughed together at that.

Just then, the three guys appeared at our table.

"There you are," Jackie said to them.

I hugged Scott and James, while Jackie hugged Bart.

"It's good to see you guys," I sincerely exclaimed.

Bart sat down on the other side of Jackie. Scott sat next to me as James sat on the other side of him.

"We already ordered, so it'll be here soon," Jackie informed them.

Four of the five of us had known one another for many years, having met while in our late twenties while swing dancing to live big bands at Glen Echo Park outside the Capital Beltway in Maryland. Once a month on Saturdays in the spring, summer, and fall, a nineteen-piece swing orchestra would assemble and blast out 1940s big band swing, while we would dance and sweat and then sweat some more in the big restored ballroom. We bonded then—and it stuck.

With Jackie an artist, Scott a software developer, and James a reporter for the *Washington Post*, the four of us were a good mix of liveliness. Bart joined our group later, when he started dating Jackie. He was an attorney, arrogant, and a control freak, but Jackie had been in love with him for years. That was enough for me to reluctantly accept his presence in our group.

We each talked about how work was going for us. Bart acted impressed that someone asked me to speak at a conference. He was all about the outward appearance of things. I overlooked that. Things seemed to be going par for the course for everyone, but something didn't feel quite right about our group's vibe. I couldn't put a finger on it, though.

Our food came about then. My stomach grumbled when I smelled the spicy platter. We feasted, with some cross banter here and there. Mostly, we were all in our own world of food and spice and delight.

Scott started talking about a program he was writing, but no one listened but me, since I was the only one who understood what he was talking about.

"Why is it that no one ever wants to hear about what I'm working on?" he asked, slightly stilted when he realized no one was listening.

Everyone paused from eating.

"Because no one—except Ann—understands your geek-talk. And she's just listening to be polite, because it's boring," Jackie blurted out. He looked affronted, and she attempted to apologize. "I'm sorry, Scott, you know I love you," she offered, making kissing noises toward him.

Scott feigned being offended. He was used to that sort of treatment.

"Well *I've* been working on this big story at the *Post*. It's probably one of the biggest I've ever dug up," James interjected.

"Do tell," I pleaded, interested in the excitement of my old life as a journalist.

"Sorry. This one's closed for discussion," James said.

"Then why did you say anything?" Jackie scolded.

"I'm just sayin'—I've got a hot iron in the fire."

We laughed.

"Well, as long as it's just an iron," I joked. "Now I know what isn't quite right," I suddenly added. "For years and years, every time we've sat down at this table, we've discussed politics and government control...but not one word of it tonight. What's going on?"

Silence. Stern faces.

"What?" I asked, looking to everyone.

More silence.

"I'll talk to you later," Jackie said quietly to me.

"Do I have a booger on my face or something? 'Cause you all are acting strange," I teased them.

Only Scott laughed.

"Well at least you laughed," I said, looking at him.

"Bart, why don't you tell us what you've been working on?" Jackie prodded, obviously changing the subject.

Bart started talking about his legislative work for a politician on Capitol Hill, sure that it made him important. His monologue lasted fifteen minutes. Unable to restrain my sour expression for any longer, I excused myself for a leisurely trip to the ladies' room. I took my time washing and drying my hands, but when I returned, Bart was still droning on. Everyone but Jackie was horribly bored.

We finished dinner, vowing to get together again soon, which of course was impossible, since I lived on the other coast.

As we left the Red Sea, Jackie discreetly passed me a note. I quickly read it.

Someone's asking questions about you.
Government. FBI?
They want to know about you going to China.

After reading the note, I made eye contact with Jackie.

But I didn't go, I wanted to say. *What's going on here? I didn't do anything.*

Jackie shrugged her shoulders as a response to my silent frustration as we all walked toward the metro station.

So that's why no one was talking politics tonight, I thought, making the connection.

Everyone hugged their goodbyes at the station entrance; I was taking a cab back down the street to my hotel.

Jackie hugged me and whispered, "Be careful."

I hugged her hard in response. She cast me one more worried look and headed off with the others.

As I hailed a cab and was driven back to my hotel, I reread the note. It was time to call Bob Hadley.

CHAPTER 20
WASHINGTON, D.C.
THE YEAR 2015

I called the clandestine switchboard, leaving my name and number for Bob, explaining that it was urgent.

I hope he's not dead. It had been a while.

The last I heard, Bob had retired, but when you spend as many years as he had with the Agency, he couldn't have possibly retired. The CIA owned him. *Or did he own them*? I wondered.

He called me an hour later.

"You interrupted my golf game, Ann," the gruff voice scolded.

"You're probably not any good anyway," I bantered.

"Wanna meet?" he asked.

"Yep."

"Secure?" he asked, wondering if I was going to talk about classified information.

"Not necessary."

"You know where Gravelly Point is?" Bob asked.

"Yeah, by Reagan National Airport, right?"

"Yes. I'll see you there at a quarter past the hour."

"Thanks, Bob."

"I said my door was always open."

"So you did. I guess there's no expiration date on that. See you in a bit."

Lulu and I quickly hopped in the rental car to head out to the George Washington Memorial Parkway in Virginia. It was normally only a fifteen-minute drive. We pulled into the parking area a few minutes early, right as a Boeing 757 took off one hundred feet over our heads, flying at one hundred and fifty miles per hour.

What a rush.

"You picked a good spot, Bob. No one's gonna hear us here," I said out loud to Lulu, who howled at the plane. I laughed.

I first visited Gravelly Point when I was in my twenties. I was with a bunch of friends, and we came to the Point during airplane rush hour. Just four hundred feet from the end of runway 1/19 at Reagan National Airport, passenger jets took off every one to two minutes at rush hour, and sometimes you could hear a vibration crackle off the Potomac River when the water was calm. We would spread blankets on the roofs of our cars and then watch the jets fly overhead. The power of the jet engines would make the cars vibrate. It was a cheap thrill.

In the middle of my flashback, Bob drove up.

Time to get serious.

Bob got out of his car, saw me, and kissed me on the cheek. That surprised me.

I smiled at him. He was larger around the middle, with more wrinkles, but the same kind brown eyes I had known.

"You look older," I played.

"You look beautiful," he countered.

"Okay, so maybe you don't look older," I teased.

He peered into my eyes. "I'm sorry about Armond," he softly offered.

"Yeah. Thank you," I said quietly.

He took my arm, and tucking it into his, we slowly started walking out of the parking lot toward the park.

"Tell me, Ann—why did you interrupt a retired old man's morning golf game to watch planes?" he inquired, just before one roared overhead.

I paused to gather my thoughts and let the plane pass.

"I flew in from Bellingham two days ago. Tomorrow I'm supposed to speak at the annual conference for the Society for Technical Communication. Last night I had dinner with some old friends, and as we're leaving the restaurant, one of them hands me this note," I said, passing him Jackie's note.

"Doesn't it rain a lot up there?" he asked.

"Where?"

"Bellingham."

"Yes."

"I thought so."

"What's that got to do with some government dweeb poking around my friends, asking about a trip to China?" I asked, irritated.

"Nothing."

"Bob, what's going on?"

"Let me guess. You didn't go to China?"

"No."

"Did you happen to dream about it?"

"Yep. Twice. Quite remarkable, both times."

"I think we'd better sit down at that picnic table over there, and you'd better tell me."

I told him in detail about my Shanghai dreams and how I'd awakened to the reality of the earthquake.

"Is there anything else about it that you intentionally didn't tell me, Ann?"

I paused.

"Yes. It's a doozy, too."

"You and I have had lots of those in our years together, haven't we?"

"Yep."

"Why should now be any different?"

"Good point," I said. "Okay, prepare yourself."

"I was born prepared, sweetheart."

"Whoa there," I cautioned, teasing.

I reached to my neck to the Herkimer diamond there, pulled the chain off, and handed him the crystal. I then explained about how I'd carried it through my dream into reality. His face registered the event—very unusual for Bob.

"So it's crossing over?" he asked.

"What is?" I asked, immediately feeling apprehensive.

"Your dreaming subconscious is crossing into your conscious reality," he quietly explained, intently staring at me as though he'd just delivered some very bad news.

We sat together as airplanes blasted overhead, followed by the wind. I pondered Bob's statement.

"I saw him, you know," I said, temporarily changing the subject.

"Saw who?" he said, then paused. "Oh, John O'Brien?" he asked, already knowing.

"Yeah. When I learned that he'd become mentally unbalanced, my heart sunk. I didn't believe that he was really ill, so I went to see him in that horrible place."

"St. Elizabeth's."

"Yeah. How can they even call it a hospital?"

The question had no answer, and we sat in silence for a moment.

"When I saw John, he told me about partial humans hatching from eggs and how human females were being implanted with alien DNA. It was all crazy talk. He was so paranoid, that he tried to carry on our entire conversation in the Gaelic, because he said that aliens were listening. I could see for myself, then, that he was ill. I had worked side by side with John for all those years. It was a different man I saw at St. Elizabeth's. When I left him that day, I told him—in the Gaelic, "Tá mo chroí istigh ionat! Go dté tú slán."

"My heart is within you. May you go safely," Bob interpreted.

"I never saw him again, and he died from a heart attack four months later."

"I know."

"In all those years, I never knew that remote viewing could be dangerous. Back then, no one ever said anything. It wasn't until five years after I left your project, when Grace died young of a heart attack without any history of heart disease in her family, that I started to consider that maybe there was a link."

Bob nodded. "Besides you, Grace was the most gifted. But there were others, and they all..." he paused. "They all died unexpectedly young from cancers or heart disease."

I looked at Bob. "That's when I started to research the effects of sensory overload."

"Too much sensory information physically stresses the body. It's similar to constant exposure to loud noise or bright lights," Bob added.

Of course he already knew about it.

After pausing while another plane soared by, I added, "I've read some scientific reports on superstring theory, where all particles and all natural forces are explained as vibrations of tiny strings. Do you know about that, too?"

"Yes. The work we were doing actually taps into a universal awareness of energy that vibrates everywhere without stopping. Perhaps when our brains tapped into that vibration, we were opening a door that is closed for a reason," he said reluctantly.

"I can see you, too, have been doing your research."

"I feel responsible for some of this."

I looked at him; he looked sad.

"For John and Grace, and all the others who died, none had any psychic experiences from childhood that they ever told me about. I, on the other hand, have been experiencing astral projection since I was a little girl, before I ever knew what it was. When you combine that with the vivid dreams I've been having since I was very young, I may have learned how to manage that unconscious-to-conscious door in my mind. Did I ever tell you that when I was trained, none of it ever seemed new to me? It was a natural extension of everything I had already been doing since I was young."

"No, you never did."

I continued, careful not to voice any classified information. "But Grace and John were artificially taught. Perhaps opening that door was just too much for them to manage. What we did there was altering the process of reality in our brains. I think our work became destructive for them when their bodies created a defense. I think that the challenge of old processes of the brain versus the new ones created a war within them. It became harmful inside, even though nothing harmful was actually occurring. Looking back now, I can see that John must have had some feeling that I would be in danger, when he so vehemently argued against me going live after only a year in training. At the time, I thought he was being controlling and overprotective. But now I wonder if it was something else. Maybe he had started to feel mentally unstable then. Do you remember how he started speaking more and more of the Gaelic as time wore on?"

"I remember."

"I just didn't know then. I was so young."

"You were never young, Ann. You were always an old soul."

"Did you know then that we were killing ourselves with that training?"

"Of course not," he said, shaking his head sadly, then pausing. "But there was something. I felt that we had to be very careful. I had a feeling that we needed to find specially gifted individuals—like you. But at some point, near my retirement, I began to be overruled by others…who thought that anyone could be trained. These other directors thought that the less emotion the person had, the more successful they would be. But after years of training, it was a disaster. Then…the deaths began," Bob confided.

"Didn't you ever wonder if I would be one of those?"

"No. Not for a nanosecond, Ann. I knew better. It was a feeling in my gut. I knew that you could manage the doorway."

"And now…what do you think now? After what I told you today about Shanghai and the crystal?" I asked pointedly.

"I told you."

"You told me what?" I asked, getting frustrated by his vagueness.

"It's crossing over. Your dreaming subconscious is crossing over into your conscious reality. The door is open, Ann, swinging back and forth, opening equally in both directions," he explained, watching me as I tried to comprehend what he was saying.

There was a foreboding look of sadness in his eyes. I could not look away.

The doorway moves in both directions.

Bob agreed to poke around to find out what the FBI wanted of me and to get back to me.

He led me to my car. When we reached it, he turned to me.

"There is something *special* in the way your mind works, Ann. I am an old man—my days here are numbered—but you…there is much you can accomplish," he said with intensity.

"You okay?"

"Yeah."

"You're not dying or anything?"

"Nope."

"Well okay, then," I said, then reached to hug him.

He hugged me hard.

I lectured at the conference the next day and schmoozed with the board members and attendees at a dinner that night, to the benefit of AlterHydro. The entire evening, though, all I could think about was remote viewing and the way it had ended my CIA friends' lives. My own involvement in it had altered the course of my life. If the doorway in my mind really swung both ways, then that meant that my dreams could now come through the door and become reality. No longer would my dreams simply be unconscious manifestations of my conscious reality—no matter how vivid they were.

I ached for the simplicity of life. I still ached for those perfect days sailing in the San Juans with Armond and Elinor.

CHAPTER 21

THE SAN JUAN ARCHIPELAGO THE YEAR 2010

We had bought her for six thousand dollars and had just finished the refit. We named her the Woohoo, after our practice of screaming the word when the sailboat would suddenly heel in unexpected wind. She was a twenty-six-foot Ranger sloop built in 1972—very well cared for, but in need of updating for the current century. Armond was passionate about buying a Gary Mull-designed sailboat after meeting Gary several years before. Armond called him one of the best storytellers he had ever known.

Aside from his near worship of the boat's designer, Armond loved the weekend pocket cruiser's qualities as well. It had all the features of larger boats, with the additional bonus of single-handling capability. What Armond loved most, though, was her speed. The Ranger 26 had won the North American IOR half-ton race in 1970, which Armond could never stop talking about, and the boat was still competitive in races now. What I liked best about the Ranger was that there was a dedicated space for the enclosed toilet, which even had a genuine teak privacy door. I also liked the wide eight-and-a-half-foot beam, which made the cabin roomy enough for various activities below deck.

Preparing the *Woohoo* for this century required money, time, and sweat equity. We were fortunate that my uncle was willing to help us. He said he was retired and bored. Our alternative energy on board included a three-hundred-watt marine wind turbine, which worked perfectly when *Woohoo* was being sailed windward, but the output would drop off a lot when she sailed downwind. We installed a towed water generator, powered through a rotor on the end of a ten-foot line. It produced nine to eleven amps constantly when sailing downwind at eight to nine knots, and this solved our power issue. After we finished all the major work, which took the entire winter and spring, we named and christened her. The day we relaunched *Woohoo*, we were thirty thousand dollars poorer, but we were gleeful with our accomplishment and her beauty.

With our aunt and uncle and all our friends there to record the event from the Squalicum Harbor boat launch, we all screamed "Woohoo!" in unison as she launched after the christening. Armond, Elinor, and I set sail for the San Juan Islands from Bellingham the morning of July tenth. Our first destination was Sucia Island, part of the Northern Boundary Islands, so called because they are the northwesternmost islands in the continental United States.

The San Juan Archipelago is a cluster of seven hundred and forty-three large and small rocky islands in the northwest corner of the continental United States. The cluster spreads north of the Strait of Juan de Fuca and south of the Boundary Pass in Canada. We motored across Bellingham Bay and past Lummi Island, then hoisted our mainsail up for the scenic Hale Passage, about twenty nautical miles south of the Canadian border, with a southwesterly prevailing wind.

As we approached Matia Island, we saw seals sunning themselves on the rocks of Puffin Island, and the three of us enjoyed watching them for as long as we could. Past Matia was Sucia Island. We arrived at Sucia in the afternoon and picked up a mooring ball in Fossil Bay. Elinor and I went below deck to prepare dinner, while Armond battened things down up top. I first pulled out the paper solar lanterns from their storage space, expanded them, and gave them to Elinor to carry up to her dad to hang on the boom for ambient light. We all took our life jackets off. We had a family rule that we all had to wear them any time we were under sail or motoring, just in case one of us was knocked into the water unexpectedly. They didn't seem necessary when we were docked.

Thirty minutes later, we ate our dinner of assorted cheese and crackers, a tossed salad, and warm apple cider in the cockpit under the boom lanterns, as we talked about our day of sailing. After dinner, we cleaned up and played Scrabble together, giving Elinor some help, although she did quite well without it. A couple of hours later, the three of us stargazed in the cool, clear night while lying on the cockpit cushions. Armond was a gifted storyteller, and he had been planning to tell us the history of Sucia Island. With warm apple cider in our hands, we were ready.

"The main island of Sucia measures over five hundred acres," he began.

"Wow, that's big," commented Elinor.

"You're right, lovey," he responded.

"There are only four residents of the island, though. Sucia Island is actually designated as a park within the Washington State Marine Park system, so there's no community here—it's just nature. If you're on the north shore of the island, there are steep cliffs that drop straight into the water. The rest of the island shore has coves and caves. You know about the Lummi Indians, right Elinor?"

"Yes, Daddy."

"There are shell middens around the island that prove that the Lummi Indians used this island."

"I forget what middens are," Elinor said.

"It's a mound of mussel shells that is very old. Finding middens here proves that native people used the island for thousands of years before other people ever found it. Also, the Lummi's used to hunt seals here once a year."

"They didn't eat them, did they? 'Cause that's kinda gross."

Armond and I laughed.

"Yes, lovey, I think they did. But I'm sure they used every part of the seals and didn't waste any of it."

"Well, I guess they could've thrown the guts and other gross stuff overboard from their canoes, and that would feed the fish," Elinor reasoned.

"I do know that they made pouches from seal fur, and they would put salmon eggs in there."

"Cool."

"In the 1900s, a thousand workers came here to mine the stone to pave the streets of Seattle. They finally realized that sandstone was too soft for streets and abandoned the mining. Sometimes you can find fossils in the sandstone here while exploring rock formations, because the rock is soft."

"Oh, that's really cool. I want to find a fossil," Elinor yearned.

"Tomorrow we'll go ashore in our dinghy to go hiking. You can look for fossils. Sucia has great trails that go through evergreen forests and wetlands. We can go beachcombing, which your mom loves."

"Oh, it's gonna be so fun."

"You're right. It'll be great fun, sweetie," I agreed, smiling.

Armond continued telling stories long into the night.

We slept peacefully in the V-berth in *Woohoo's* bow, snuggled together in our double sleeping bag, while Elinor slept on the long cushion on the starboard side of the main cabin. The boat rocked gently with the tide.

That night I dreamed of skiing with Armond and Elinor at Mount Baker near Bellingham, and in the dream I couldn't find Armond. Elinor and I were looking for him everywhere. There was a storm—a whiteout—and Elinor and I took shelter in the lodge, but

Armond was not with us. We were both crying and afraid, and I didn't understand why I couldn't find him. I awoke with a start, sitting bolt upright in the V-berth, hitting my head in the process.

"Are you okay?" Armond asked sleepily.

"I had a horrible dream. We were skiing on Mount Baker, and I couldn't find you anywhere."

"Oh, come here. It's okay, babe," he said, pulling me close.

"I think this was a warning dream," I said in his ear, remembering the eerie dream. "I need to get you an emergency beacon before we go skiing again," I whispered to him.

"Okay—we'll get it, then," he agreed.

"It was horrible. Elinor and I were so sad and afraid," I said to him, near tears.

"It's gonna be okay, babe. It's gonna be okay," he reassured me, holding me firm.

It took me half the next day before I could shake the terrible feeling I had.

We spent the next two days hiking and beachcombing Sucia, and Elinor was elated to find three fossils. Each night, we stayed on the island long enough to witness the sunsets, which started with pinks, then purples, and then ended in bright orange colors. Just before it all left, we would get into the dingy and motor back to the *Woohoo*, seeing the colors reflecting off the calm sea like a mirror.

We left Sucia to make our way to North Pender Island in British Columbia, about eleven nautical miles west of Sucia. Because of the winds and currents, we ended up doing a lot of tacking and sail adjustments. The going was slow, so Armond pulled up the dinghy, and Elinor and I climbed down the transom ladder into it, while Armond clipped himself into the cockpit for safety. He steered *Woohoo* while Elinor and I had a two-hour ride together in the dinghy. It was wonderful on a day of slow sailing. Late in the afternoon, we entered Otter Bay Marina from the Swanson Channel.

Elinor and I set to showering on shore, and then we washed clothes while Armond settled our moorage, topped off our water-storage tank, and looked over the *Woohoo.* We had dinner at the marina after we had all showered. During the meal, we decided that the next day we'd hire someone to help us explore North Pender Island's coastline in kayaks.

Ned Hawkins was an expert kayak guide whose recommendation preceded him. Ned insisted that Elinor kayak with him, and Armond and I took the second vessel together. We were not disappointed when we discovered seals, herons, and five separate sightings of bald eagles. Our trip turned to pure joy, however, when we were joined by harbor porpoises and then a little later by Dall's porpoises. After Ned explained the difference between the two, it was easy to identify the Dall's porpoises because of their uniquely thick bodies and small heads, as well as the white markings on their flanks. Their coloring resembled that of Orcas. The peak of our expedition came, though, when we spotted a pod of Orcas from our kayaks.

"Orcas!" Ned shouted like he suddenly had a bullhorn. "Kayak paddles up," he instructed sharply.

We all lifted our paddles, then froze as he'd shown us before we started.

The killer whales seemed huge from our low vantage point. Ned reached forward and gave Elinor's shoulder a squeeze and said something to her. I immediately was appreciative that he had insisted that Elinor kayak with him. As we drifted together silently, the pod of seven came very close, within about ten feet of us. I couldn't believe how straight and tall their dorsal fins were. Ned pointed out a very large male. It was about twenty-five feet long, with a dorsal fin that must have reached over five feet high. I watched in awe as it smoothly swam past us, both breathtaking and frightening at the same time. The black and white of its shiny skin, the way the salt water slid from its sides…I knew this was something I would always remember.

I glanced toward Elinor, and I could tell she felt the same way. In all the years that Armond and I had kayaked the islands, we had never seen an Orca from the water. Armond reached to me and took my hand in his, linking us forever in this snapshot of time. For the few minutes that the pod swam near us, I marveled at the adventure I'd never expected to have. As the Orcas moved away, Ned explained that the core Orca habitat is the entire Georgia Basin, which included the South Puget Sound, the Strait of Juan de Fuca, Rosario Strait, Georgia Strait, and the entire San Juan Islands. The whales travel in large groups, chasing salmon in the summer months.

Later, I asked Elinor what Ned had said to her when he squeezed her shoulder. He had said, "Prepare yourself for the most beautiful sight you'll ever see."

He was right.

We were high after that experience—none of us could stop smiling. We spent the next two days exploring North Pender Island, swimming in the heated pool at the marina, and eating.

On the third day, we headed out.

We were fortunate to catch a tide on our route back to Bellingham harbor. *Woohoo's* theoretical hull speed was six knots, but we were able to hit nine knots when we sailed in the current. It was a wild, fun, exhilarating, and fast sail back to Bellingham.

CHAPTER 22

BELLINGHAM, WASHINGTON THE YEAR 2015

Remembering those perfect days was a balm to me. When Armond was alive, I was cocooned in his trust and protection. I felt that nothing could harm me when I was with him. Remembering those perfect days in the San Juan Islands, I could now see that my dreams were warning me even then.

Bob called me on my cell phone just after I arrived in Bellingham from the Washington, D.C. conference.

"Ann?"

"Hi, Bob. Good timing; I just got in."

"Everything go okay on the flight?"

"You mean besides the fact that the TSA is completely out of their mind?" I exclaimed.

"Did something happen?"

"I got shuffled into the see-through-your-clothes x-ray machine at the airport," I said sarcastically.

"Oh, is that all?"

"Nope, that's not all. You gotta hear this."

"Okay."

"I get through the obnoxious machine, and I'm standing next to the conveyer, putting all my electronics away, and I hear these TSA guys talking. I look over, and these two dweebs are hitting the color and enhance button whenever women pass through the machine. A couple of perverts. Then, as I keep watching, I see one guy look at his boss, who is standing just behind them, and he turns to him and says, 'Two.' The boss looks over at the next person in line, who is a huge Tongan-looking man, and the boss says, 'Three and you're on.'"

"What?" Bob asked.

"Listen. So the first guy says, 'Twenty bills.' The boss nods yes. When the Tongan comes into the scanner, the two TSA guys and their boss lean forward, looking at the screen closely. The boss says, 'One…two.' He's counting. One TSA guy tells the Tongan to raise his arms above his head. The boss again says, 'One…two…three.' And the TSA guy dejectedly passes his boss a twenty. Then I realize what they're betting on, Bob. It was the fat rolls on the guy," I exclaimed.

"Oh brother. The TSA have never been the brightest bulbs in the pack. You know that."

"I couldn't believe it. And these are the guys that are supposed to be protecting us from another 9-11."

"The TSA are *babysitters*, nothing more," Bob replied.

"Anyway, enough about our national voyeur security. Did you find out anything about my pursuers?"

"Yes, I did learn a few things."

"Yeah, what?"

"First, the project is still live."

"What? Did you know about that, Bob?" I accused.

"No, I didn't. I had no idea. It was moved to another agency, like I told you in D.C. And I think you know which agency it went to, Ann."

"The only one that cared about it."

"Yes."

"Are they the ones who've been asking my friends why I was in that other place we spoke about?"

"Well, kind of. They sent private contractors. So it's *not* them, but it *is* them."

"Oh great."

"Ann, I think I've persuaded them that the information they received was faulty and that you weren't there. So none of your friends should be hearing from them anymore."

I sighed in relief. "One thing I remembered that I didn't tell you before was that I thought I saw a man."

"Where?"

"In my dream, right after I found the crystal."

"Explain it to me."

"Well, I picked up the Herkimer and realized what it was to me, and then I thought I saw a man out of the corner of my eye, and when I turned that way to get a look at him, he wasn't there. It felt strange."

There was no response from Bob.

"Bob?"

"I'm here."

"Well?"

"It was someone live, Ann."

"Looking at me?"

"Yes."

A remote viewer was watching me dream?

"We need to be careful with this part," Bob said, discreetly warning me about discussing classified information on an unsecured line.

"Okay."

"Do you remember your first day going live?"

"Of course."

"Do you remember the coordinates?"

"I think I can recall them."

"Remember those skills we taught you. They will help you now."

"Okay."

"When you do so, Ann, take the information and compare it to the recent earthquake. Do that. You might come up with something interesting."

"All right," I agreed.

"Be careful," he warned me.

"Of what?"

"Sweet dreams. Remember that. Do you have people you can trust there?" he asked, sounding worried.

"I have one, maybe two here."

"Find out. Confirm it. If not, remember you've got me, but I'm pretty far away."

"Well I hope I won't need anyone's help."

He paused.

"I hope so too, Ann."

After hanging up, I thought about the phone call for a while. I first tried to reason through what I knew so far. The remote-viewing project was still live—but at another government agency. If another group had Project Stargate, it meant that it was being used, because we'd already proven that it worked. So they were likely using it on active targets. They were using it knowing that it would kill most of the viewers.

They'd had a viewer active while I was dreaming of being in Shanghai. Of everything, that probably scared me the most. I had just discovered the now non-existent boundary between my conscious and subconscious minds. The new remote-viewing group, it seemed, had found the connection much earlier, and I was reaching to understand the implications. The new viewers could see my dreams as if they were with me—as if they were viewing the same location at the same time I was dreaming.

I've lost my anonymity. I felt sick. I barely made it to the toilet in time before everything inside my guts turned inside out. Sitting on the bathroom rug, I thought. *I've worked for so long to maintain my privacy. I deserve it. Now, every time I dream, they could be watching me.* I was starting to get angry.

Getting up, I washed my face and brushed my teeth, then went in my bedroom, kicked off my shoes, and crawled into bed. Emotionally exhausted and deeply drained, I fell asleep.

I woke up soon after, fear spearing through me. My face felt sweaty, and I looked around the room for the threat, but then I remembered: the threat was in my mind. Had I dreamed? I looked at the clock and saw that I had only dozed off for a little over a half hour. I didn't remember dreaming.

It had been twenty years since I'd tried to remote view. I tried to tell myself that it was like getting back on a horse after being bucked off.

But horses don't generally inflict an early death on their riders.

I was nervous, but I decided that now was as good a time as any to remount.

Moving to the living room, I sat on the sofa with my clipboard and pencil, preparing myself to start the Transcendental Meditation. Even after I'd left Project Stargate, I practiced TM and had found it to be an extremely effective tool for reducing stress in my life. After Armond's death, I even attended an Ayurvedic healing retreat at the clinic on Salt Spring Island in the San Juans. They taught me that TM could open an infinite reservoir of creativity and intuitive intelligence. I became even more devoted to meditating after that, practicing it daily.

After twenty minutes of meditation, I slowly opened my eyes to the clipboard paper and wrote the time and the word BEGIN. I then imagined that day, twenty-five years ago, when I conducted my first live remote view.

On my paper, I drew the large remote-viewing room at the CIA, where small groups of people sat quietly, all with clipboards in their laps. I sketched a man sitting, with another man sitting behind him. There was also a woman. The man nearest the woman handed her a piece of paper. On that paper were numbers…coordinates. I wrote them down.

Latitude: N 31° 14' 10.7712
Longitude: E 121° 29' 9.9126

Finished, I wrote END, along with the current time. I had successfully viewed my original target coordinates. The feeling of being a passive observer of my own self *in the past* was surreal.

"Sinéad, tell me the latitude and longitude for the epicenter of the Shanghai earthquake."

She began, "Latitude: N 31° 14' 10.7712, Longitude: E 121° 29' 9.9126"

"Stop." The coordinates were the same. *Oh my goodness. My first live target at the CIA was the Bund Hotel.* Did I see the future, or did I create it? Did the swinging door in my mind carry my subconscious to reality and, through my dream, generate the epicenter of the earthquake at the Bund?

The phone rang, pulling me away from my thoughts.

"Sinéad, take a message," I abruptly instructed her. I wasn't ready to talk to anyone. After a few moments, the phone stopped ringing.

"Message ready, Ann."

"Replay the message."

"Ann…it's Paul. I know you're back from D.C. Now…about that date…"

"Stop."

My brain was tired. I didn't want to deal with this right now. Then I thought of Bob's reminder. I needed to know whom I could trust. It would have been easy to tell myself that didn't apply to Paul…but I wasn't sure anymore.

"Sinéad, dial Paul from the number he called me from. Send the call to my cell phone."

"Okay, Ann."

The phone rang, and I heard Paul pick up. "Hello?"

"Hi, Paul. It's Ann."

"Hey there."

"I was glad you called," I said flatly.

"Are you okay? You sound…different. Did everything go okay at the conference?"

"The conference was fine. Would you like to come over? I could fix us a late dinner."

"Yeah, I can be right over," he responded.

"Okay."

"Ann?"

"Yeah?"

"You might need to tell me where you live. My telepathy isn't quite working tonight," he teased, trying to cheer me up.

He has no idea.

CHAPTER 23
BELLINGHAM, WASHINGTON
THE YEAR 2015

I threw together a green salad for us, with broiled organic chicken and roasted walnuts on top with Caesar dressing. Cooking was always good for centering myself.

That'll have to do.

About twenty minutes later, the doorbell rang.

I went to the door and opened it.

Paul was dressed in a Bellslicker, a white t-shirt, and stone-colored boot-cut Levi's. With his casual look, he wore a big smile and presented a bouquet of wildflowers from his hand.

"Beautiful," I said, impressed by the flowers.

"Me or the flowers?" he asked playfully, returning my smile.

"Both," I said, stepping aside so he could enter. My heart leapt just a bit.

"Thank you, Paul," I said sincerely, holding the flowers in one arm while I hugged him with the other.

He kissed me on the cheek just as we pulled apart.

That was a surprise…but a pleasant one. I liked his forwardness.

"How about we sit up here and eat?" I suggested, gesturing to the tall chairs at the kitchen island.

Seeing the salad and bread, he replied, "Mmm…looks good."

He sat while I put the wildflowers in a vase, setting it on the counter.

I dished up salad, bread, and pink lemonade for both of us.

"So why don't you tell me what's up? I could hear something in your voice when you called me back."

"You get straight to the point, don't you?" I asked, coming around the counter to sit next to him.

"Ann, I've been working next to you five days a week for three years. That's…" he was clearly calculating in his mind, "…seven hundred and eighty days I've spent with you. We're a little past small talk now, don't you think?"

"Wow, you're really good at math," I said while winking, glazing over his question.

"Ha ha."

For a moment I looked directly into my salad as though looking for something. I was gathering my thoughts.

"I sure hope you're ready for this, because it's a doozy," I warned, forking my salad.

"Bring it on."

"I used to work for the CIA. Did you know that?"

"Nope, didn't know that. How long ago?" he asked, looking into his salad.

I recounted the story of how I started working there. He nodded as he ate, indicating that he was still following me.

"So," I said, "I was there for a total of six and a half years."

"That's a long time. What'd you do for them? Were you a spy—Bond?" he kidded.

"Yes, I was," I replied seriously.

A piece of chicken fell off his fork. "Really?"

"Yeah, but not in the way that you imagine. I never physically went into the field."

"Well that's good. What did you do?"

"I worked from CIA headquarters, in Langley. I was part of the Science and Technology group, in Clandestine Services. Our group developed the methods and technology to improve how we gathered intelligence. It's the same organization that develops all the cool spy gadgets, like what James Bond uses."

"That is cool," he said with eyebrows raised.

"Of course you would think so, you geek," I teased.

He smiled. The way we interacted with one another was easy. I decided to dive into the more complicated stuff.

"Can I ask you something?" I asked quietly.

"Yeah, ask me anything."

"What do you think of our government?"

"The U.S. Government?"

"Yeah."

"Well, if we're gonna get into politics, I need to know how old you are."

"What?" I asked, laughing.

"Tell me how old you are."

"Why? How old do you think I am?"

"Did the CIA teach you how to answer a question with another question?" he teased.

I laughed.

"No. As a matter of fact, I developed that myself—over forty-four years of lifetime."

"Forty-four? Really? I could have sworn you were under thirty-five."

"Yeah, I get that a lot," I said, showing off.

"Boy, you've got good genes," he said, impressed.

"My mother had good skin."

"I bet. Well now that I know you're forty-four…" He winked. "You and I are the same age."

"Really?"

"Uh-huh. It helps to know your age, because I can see where you're coming from, knowing what period of time you've lived in."

"I can see that. It gives context."

"Yes, it does. Are you sure you want to know my opinion of our government? I mean, I've never worked for the government, nor would I ever. My feelings may be very different than yours."

"Yes. I asked because I want to know."

"I'm a patriot, Ann. I believe in this country," he began.

I noticed that his face changed as he started. There was no more bantering. It was all seriousness.

"But I don't believe in the socialization that's been happening since about 2009. I'm against our government using RFID, whether it's tracking animals, our medical records, or us. Local government, at the county and city levels, has become a noose around the neck of its citizens. The astronomical property and other local taxes are just plain wrong. The county foreclosed on my neighbor's house for two thousand that he owed in back taxes, and his house is worth at least three hundred thousand dollars. I have another friend whose house is on a big piece of land, and yet he can't keep livestock on his own land. His daughter wants to have chickens so that she can participate in 4H, and they are forbidden by the city to do so. They have sixteen acres, Ann. What happened to 'we the people?'" He was getting fired up.

I nodded. I had never seen this side of him; he seemed so different.

Paul continued, "You know I love technology, but the things that all levels of government are doing with it is just plain wrong. We need change, from the highest levels of government."

He paused, waiting for my reaction to his confession.

"I agree with every single word you just spoke," I said, looking intently into his eyes.

He met my eyes, then reached toward me and kissed me, full on the lips. I kissed him back. He gently stopped, leaning his forehead to mine. I told myself to breathe; the chemistry was palpable.

He backed his head slightly away from mine and, looking into my eyes, said, "I knew you were beautiful, Ann. But I think you just became even more so."

"Mmmm," I responded, unable to find any coherent words.

He smiled.

I drank my lemonade.

He drank his and then ate a little salad.

"I have a good friend who lives in a tiny city in Eastern Washington, and she can't have chickens on her farm, and she lives on eleven acres," I offered, trying to break the lively tension between us.

"I'd like to take a million dollars, hire an attorney, and sue the crap outta that city, just for her right to keep some hens for fresh eggs."

"Her neighbor just turned her in to the county because they found a noxious weed on her farm. Now the noxious-weed person from the county is harassing her, saying that his team will come onto her farm and spray it with pesticides to kill the weeds and then charge her for it. So my friend got out her shovel and dug up those weeds, and now the county tells her that she'll remain on their list forever and that they'll be coming to her farm every year to inspect whether the weed is eradicated."

"That's insanity," Paul exclaimed.

"It is. What's incredibly ironic is that her county is millions short in their budget, and yet that noxious-weed person has a full-time job—harassing people like her. That job should be eliminated."

"That's exactly what I'm talking about. The harassment of individual citizens is an epidemic. Did you know there could be neighbors, right now in this neighborhood, who could be listening to our conversation by having the right equipment they bought off the web? I consider it my constitutional right to have my privacy, and yet we're losing it."

"Peekers."

"Yes, peekers. So you know about them?" he asked.

"I do."

"Mmm, that's interesting. You're an interesting woman."

"I'll take that as a compliment."

"You should. Since we're both done picking over our dinner, do you want to sit on the couch?" he asked.

"Sure."

"So are you allowed to tell me about your work for the CIA?" he asked as we sat down facing one another.

"I can talk about some of it here, but not any specifics."

"Hmmm, okay."

"Remember the dream I told you about before I went to the conference in D.C.?"

"Yeah. You were freaked out about it, with the quartz showing up. I've thought a lot about it since then."

"You have?"

"Yeah, it was bizarre."

"I think I understand why it unnerved me."

He nodded, begging for more.

"When I was in D.C., I met with my old CIA boss."

"Tryin' to get your old job back?"

"Very funny, but no. I was trying to understand why the government sent men to my friends in D.C., asking why I was recently in Shanghai."

"You went to China? When?"

"That's the thing. I've never been to China."

"Then why did they think you had? And which part of the government was asking?"

"They were government contractors, hired by a certain agency, not the CIA. They thought I had been in China because I dreamed that I was in Shanghai."

I waited for his brain to catch up.

Silence.

He raised eyebrows…then recognition.

"No way. They saw you dreaming of Shanghai?"

"No. They saw me in Shanghai, as though I were actually there in real life."

Silence again.

He was a bit slow in wrapping his head around it.

"So you dreamed of being in Shanghai, and some government people, who presumably were spying on the same place in China, saw you. Then they started asking your friends why you were in China. The question is, what James Bond kind of technology allows them to see you as though you were there?"

"It's not technology—it's people. People who are trained to use the subconscious part of their brains to find out information, without actually being there."

"Holy cow. Is that what you used to do?"

"Yes."

"That's serious stuff. You're trained as a peeker without needing any technology."

"It doesn't exactly work like that, but I can't really explain it to you in detail. I would like to talk to you, though, about what's been happening since that dream."

"Okay."

At least he's open to listening to more, instead of running out of my house, screaming that I'm a spy.

Looking at him intently, I said, "Warning…this is the scary part."

"Go ahead," he replied steadily.

"My training was like flexing a muscle that I didn't know I had. I strengthened my subconscious and made it into a power-muscle that allowed me to travel using my mind without bounds to gather information. I was very, very good at what I did for the Agency. I was the best they had for the entire six years that I worked for them."

I paused to ensure he was following. He nodded, so I continued.

"I flexed this muscle of my subconscious, and over all these years, I guess it's been getting more and more powerful. When I had the dream of being in Shanghai, my subconscious crossed over into reality. The last thing I dreamed that night was that there was an earthquake beginning, and when I awoke, there had been. That's why the Herkimer was there with me. In my conscious mind, I was really there. The government people saw me there. And I saw someone from that dream in my real life, here."

"Here in Bellingham?"

"Well, here in the Pacific Northwest. I saw him and talked with him. He was real, and he remembered being there in Shanghai with me."

"Is that guy in the program, too?"

"I don't know."

"Hmmm."

"So you really were there—in Shanghai, I mean."

"Yes, I was—but I traveled there through my dream."

"It's kinda like teleporting," he said, shaking his head.

I nodded. I think he was starting to comprehend what I was explaining.

"I also learned something from my old CIA boss that I never knew before."

"What's that?"

"My first live target for the Agency was the same physical location that I went to in my dream. But the thing is, I never knew until he told me in D.C. this week that those coordinates were that physical location. You see, at that time I only had latitude and longitude, so I didn't know where the target was," I rushed to explain.

"That's heavy stuff, Ann."

"I know."

"Just to clarify…whatever you dream, you can manifest in reality?"

"Not always—I don't think."

"Can you control it?"

"No. I didn't even know that those coordinates from twenty-five years ago were the coordinates for the very location that I dreamed in Shanghai." I paused. "I might have killed all those people in Shanghai," I confessed, looking into his eyes.

"No you didn't," he firmly responded, reaching out to grip my shoulder.

"I dreamed of the earthquake, but I might have actually created it," I insisted, sharing my anxiety.

"You didn't. The CIA killed those people by opening your subconscious. They are responsible, not you. You can't put this on yourself. You would never do that," he argued, forcing me to look at him.

I looked back at him silently.

"Is the government still poking around your friends?" he asked me.

"No. My old CIA boss put a stop to that."

"He's still there after twenty-five years?"

"No, he's retired. Well, I guess no one ever retires from the CIA after being there so long. But he was able to convince the people who were asking the questions that they had made a mistake and that I was never there."

"Well, at least that's good news."

"It's the only piece of good news. There is one other thing I really should tell you."

"What's that?" he asked with concern.

"Every single person who did what I did for the CIA is dead."

"Dead as in killed, murdered?" he asked, stress in his voice.

"No, natural causes, all of them."

"Natural causes? What do you mean?" he asked suspiciously.

"The work we did caused psychosis in my closest friend from the project, and then he died of a heart attack a few months later. Others died of early heart attacks without having any genetic history, and some others died of unusual cancers. I'm the only original team member alive."

"But your old boss…he's alive," Paul countered.

"He ran the program, but he never…well…participated in what we were doing."

Paul's face took on a pained cast.

"I don't think I'm in danger," I responded to his worried look.

"Why?" he asked, wanting me to prove it.

"None of the others who died had the natural paranormal gifts that I do. They were all trained for the technique. But I already had it."

"What do you mean?" he asked again.

His arm rested on the back of the sofa protectively, caressing my shoulder.

"Are you familiar with astral projection?"

"Like Shirley MacLaine?" he asked with his eyebrow screwed upward.

I laughed out loud.

"What?" he asked, unable to keep a straight face.

I laughed until I was doubling over on the couch, unable to let the humor of it fall away. It brought me back to John O'Brien and how it had cracked him up when I had said it all those years ago.

"What?" he said, clearly enjoying watching me.

I started to calm myself. "Nothing. But that was just too funny. Never mind. Yes, like Shirley MacLaine."

He gave me a stern look that said I don't like not getting the joke.

I thought that was funny too—perhaps my laughter was a release of all my emotion.

I continued.

"Okay—astral projection. Since I was a young girl, I could leave my body at will. I had no idea that it was paranormal then."

He nodded.

"Also, when I was twelve years old, I had a near-death experience, brought on by an accident I had. My family was visiting friends, and their children and my sisters and I were all playing on their frozen pond, pretending to be famous ice skaters. Our friends pulled out their three-wheeled ATV, driving it over the ice. I decided to grab the handlebar on the back, and as the driver accelerated, my hand slipped off, and I flipped backward, hitting the back of my head hard on the ice. It knocked me out cold."

I looked at Paul, who nodded for me to go on.

"My spirit left my body, and I could see my body below, lying on the ice. I saw the kids move my body to the grass on the pond's edge. I fell into a coma and woke up three days later in the hospital. While I was out of my body, both at the pond and at the hospital, I had experiences that I remember."

His eyebrows went up at that. "What do you remember?"

"I was my soul, my energy, and I was separate from my physical body. That means that our bodies are not really us. Without the constraints of my physical body, I was able to float, as my spirit, watching and observing others. I heard what others thought. As my body was in the hospital bed, I floated around my room, listening to the people who were there, or I'd go into the halls and watch and listen to people as they passed by."

"Oh man. That's incredible. What did you say when you woke up from the coma?"

"Well, it was very difficult to explain. I was only twelve years old. Basically, no one believed me. My mother thought I was brain damaged. So I kept my secret. From that moment on, I knew that I didn't have to be constrained by my body."

"That must have been difficult, having no one believe you."

"It was."

"Was anything different when you recovered?"

"My dreaming became even more vivid. I mean, since I was a little girl I've had remarkable dreams, but after the accident, I noticed that bits of my dreams would sometimes come true."

Paul was nodding, and I could see that he was processing everything I was telling him.

"Perhaps because I've been dealing with the paranormal for most of my life, I am able to manage that doorway between the unconscious and conscious mind. Maybe that's why I'm alive."

"Maybe." He seemed to agree.

"My friends that I worked with all those years…maybe their minds couldn't handle that open doorway…"

"So you're the only person alive who can handle this kind of swinging doorway between the conscious and subconscious?"

"Well, from the original program, yes."

"So if you're the best at the technique, why has the government allowed you to walk free?"

"What could they gain by taking me?"

He paused, looking into my eyes. "A weapon," he replied solemnly.

CHAPTER 24

BELLINGHAM, WASHINGTON THE YEAR 2015

Our conversation dwindled to a stop soon after that. Paul could tell I was tired, so he kissed me on the forehead and left. I was tired of thinking about the CIA, remote viewing, and anything else about having been a remote spy. I just wanted to go to bed.

As I lay there, I took a deep breath and thought about what Paul had said about RFID.

Radio frequency technology had been around since Marlin Perkins hosted *Mutual of Omaha's Wild Kingdom* on television. That was in the days of rabbit-ear antennas that you had to position correctly in order to see the image on your TV, and you had to get up off the sofa to change the channel. For twenty-seven years, Perkins radio tagged animals. That's how most older Americans remembered the first use of radio frequency technology. But it was used before then by the allies in World War II, as a means of identifying whether the planes coming in were friend or foe.

The newest generation of RFID tags was called the Mu2 Chip. It was far smaller than the size of a freckle on a person's face and more than one hundred times thinner than a single piece of paper. The Japanese corporation Hitachi developed it. The tiny mini-dot stored data that could identify and track, it had no need for battery power, and it could operate in both moisture and heat. With the Mu2 chip, RFID was no longer simply a device to relay information. Now it stored information in a database where that data could be quickly and easily retrieved by computers.

RFID was a global initiative and was always kept quiet. India's secretive RFID initiative, called Aadhaar, was exposed by an article in the *Wall Street Journal* five years ago. India not only had an initiative to tag all its citizens with the Mu chip, but they also added an iris and fingerprint biometric scan to their data collection strategy and then assigned a unique twelve-digit number to every one of their 1.2 billion souls. Rice farmers and rural shop owners who had never even seen a computer or biometric scanner were awakened by officials the night before they were to report to their mobile scan center. It took the government five years and billions of dollars, but India did indeed achieve its goal. All Indian citizens could now be tracked with a Mu chip embedded in their passports, driver's licenses, ration cards, and health-insurance cards. The Indian government employed fear to convince their parliament to approve the tagging of citizens. It is that same rhetoric of fear that was used to convince governments in countries all around the world to use RFID on their citizens, including America.

In the early part of the new century, the government touted RFID's use for animal disease control, in case of mad cow disease, hoof-and-mouth disease, swine flu, avian flu, and other outbreaks. The government used the fear of pandemics to make it mandatory that all animals were chipped, including all pets. That was the first step in desensitizing the population to acceptance of RFID. Added to that was the lobbying efforts of the RFID industry—which is worth thirty billion dollars today. Those lobbyists kicked up their persuasiveness after the 9-11 attacks in 2001, using fear to convince the government that they could prevent terrorism in America by tracking everyone in the country. Out of the nineteen terrorists of 9-11, nine of them had obtained Virginia driver's licenses. After 9-11, Virginia was the first state to use terrorism fear to mandate RFID chips in its driver's licenses. After Virginia, many states followed, and then the federal government mandated that all states adopt tracking. In 2006, the United States started chipping its citizens through passports, recording the date, time, and place of entries and exits from the USA. After 2014, no one could participate in American society without an RFID. Driving a car, opening a bank account, getting a loan, buying real estate or a new car, or traveling outside the country all required RFID.

GOG was vehemently against using RFID on citizens. From the organization's perspective, civil liberties were forfeited when RFID was employed. Our individuality was lost because governments using RFID expected their citizens to live inside the box; outside-the-box citizens were flagged as noncompliant. With the power granted to the government through the technology, citizens had no second chances. With RFID, it was easy for the government to spy on its citizens domestically, because everyone's movements were charted in databases. The newest chips could be read from a few hundred feet away or by satellites, making the peeking threat easier. Peeking could be done by governments, organizations, or individuals—like stalkers who wanted to follow their prey. The GOG underground organization saw RFIDs as a means to punish citizens who didn't follow a conformist way of thinking.

In 2010, the U.S. Food and Drug Administration approved the use of RFIDs in humans, and human trials of implanted chips had begun. First the trials were voluntary. Subjects were implanted with their medical record information to supposedly speed up care in hospitals. Again the government used fear to entice citizens to voluntarily participate. Then in 2014, all violent or deviant convicted criminals were required to be implanted with an RFID upon their parole from prison, for a period of time determined by each parole board. Politicians raved about this mandate, saying it was the end to repeat offenders, especially in crimes against children. With this positive spin, the idea of chipping humans seemed viable for community safety.

Once a person was chipped, there was little escape, which was why GOG fought against it so vehemently. There were ways to disable an RFID, such as the sharp tap from a hammer or by cooking it in your microwave. But as soon as the technology was disabled, it would go offline in the government's database, and the person it belonged to was flagged for noncompliance. So far there was no viable way to disable the chip without getting caught.

What would Marlin Perkins think of tagging humans? I wondered. *Maybe it's best that he's not around to see the results.*

CHAPTER 25
BELLINGHAM, WASHINGTON
THE YEAR 2015

It was nearing my birthday, and I was dreading going to the DMV to renew my driver's license. It wasn't just the jail-like photo they would take, but the grief I felt over the loss of my privacy, knowing that I was surrendering myself to an RFID tracking chip. Not to mention the fact that dealing with DMV employees was like walking into a hive of African bees—they were just waiting for a reason to sting you.

I parked and then went into the building, took my wait-till-hell-freezes-over number, and took a seat in the third row from the back, on the end. I wanted to sit in the back row, or I would have settled for the one in front of it, but every seat was taken in the back two rows. The first eight rows were empty, with the exception of one pimply-faced high school eager beaver, who had no idea what was in store for him when he took the driving test.

Thirty-five minutes later, I heard number forty-nine called. I was up. I rose and shot for the lighted arrow, maneuvering into my lane.

"Yes?" the woman behind the counter said flatly, not making eye contact.

Would it kill her to act like a human being?

"I need my driver's license renewed," I said, impersonating her monotonous voice.

"Got the form?" she asked, still not looking up.

I passed my paper across the wide counter.

"Is this address correct?"

"Yes."

She punched some things into the computer.

"The computer says it's wrong."

"Huh?" I responded, dumbfounded.

"The computer says this address is wrong," she repeated, slower this time, as though I were dense.

"Well it's the only one I have, regardless of whether the computer likes it or not," I responded curtly.

"If it's not a valid address, you can't use it."

"It *is* a valid address."

"Todd," the woman shouted, apparently to a higher-up. "Can you come here?"

Great.

Todd approached, not looking at me, and asked the woman, "What's wrong?"

"Her address isn't valid."

"Yes it is," I countered, standing firmly.

Both Todd and the woman ignored me.

"The form says 'Lane,' and you typed in 'Street,'" Todd said.

I could have sworn I heard him mutter "you idiot" under his breath.

Todd walked away, scorning. The woman's head ducked slightly, her cheeks blooming in pink.

"Sixty-eight dollars," she demanded, averting her eyes.

I slid a hundred-dollar bill over the counter.

"Don't you have something smaller?" she asked with disgust, not touching the bill but staring at it.

"Nope," I said curtly, though I knew I did.

She took the edge of the bill and disdainfully put it in the bottom of her cash drawer and then gave me thirty-two dollars back by simply setting it on the counter. I took the money and put it in my wallet.

"Wait over there until your name is called for your photo," she said, pointing.

I waited again. No shocker there.

In fifteen minutes, my name was called to have my photo taken.

I really wanted to take a pair of those google-eyed glasses and put them on for the photo, surprising the amateur photographer, but I guessed she probably wouldn't think it was funny. I decided to go the depressed, straight-face route.

After my picture was taken, I waited again. My name was finally called, my prison photo was released, and I had my new driver's license in hand, tracking me wherever I went.

When I got into my BYD, I sat in the driver's seat and looked at the license. At a glance, it seemed perfectly harmless. But in this one piece of plastic, my civil liberties were violated, and it was mandatory in order to participate in American society. I could not drive out of the parking lot in the car that I owned free and clear without this card. As I sat there, I thought about the nameless Canadian whom I had challenged before he became a member of GOG. He'd said, "…if I attend a gun show, all a government employee has to do is hold an RFID reader nearby, and he can ID me, because my driver's license is in my wallet…this is an invasion of my privacy…" He was right. I had done nothing but serve my country faithfully, and I was being tracked just because I was an American.

I thought about what I knew about disabling RFIDs. I knew people who had disabled the tag through various methods, but the complication was that the government would know about it immediately by the driver's license number going offline. The best option was to clone your RFID chip—but the risk of being found out was high. The government had a dedicated team of developers constantly working on refining their cloning-detection software, and if you *were* found out, it was an automatic felony with prison time. None of these options seemed very appealing to me.

I felt the Herkimer diamond around my neck, removed it, and looked at it in the sunlight coming through the car window. The prisms made me think of how quartz could create an electric field, making it act like a circuit. Paul said that voltage was produced across the crystal's face, making it vibrate at a certain frequency, the crystal maintaining that constant frequency. If regular quartz crystals could be a circuit, creating a force field, and could create a frequency, could a phantom Herkimer do even more? I looked at the crystal in my hand and noticed how it was so clear, with one perfect crystal formed inside the outer one.

Can this super-charged crystal be used to disrupt RFID? I wondered, looking at the phantom Herkimer in one hand and my new driver's license in the other.

I looked at the DMV building out the car window.

All that personal information was stored in a database somewhere. I wondered if the database itself could be disrupted and corrupted using a force field created by my Herkimer. *But that would be destruction of government property*, I thought. *I could be thrown in jail for that.*

The Canadian RFID program was run the same way as ours, with a database holding personal information. I wondered if I could use remote viewing, bringing my Herkimer with me, to disrupt the Canadian RFID database and its backup. It would be my first test—if I could do it.

I pulled the safe phone out of my purse, assembled it, and placed my call to the Canadian contact number I had memorized.

"B40 for coordinates, soon," I said, leaving the message.

I set my watch timer for the four-minute window I had.

One minute later, my phone rang.

"Yes?" I answered.

"Code?"

"Salmon."

"Victoria," she confirmed.

"I need map coordinates for the B.C. driver's license data center and the backup location."

"I'll call you back."

I pulled out the small clipboard that I started carrying in my purse, along with a pencil, to record the longitude and latitude of the data centers. I'm sure they knew where the Canadian Government stored its primary database that held citizens' RFID data, but they'd have to pull up the actual coordinates, and the same for the backup data center.

My phone rang a minute later.

"Yes?"

"Code?"

"Salmon."

"Victoria."

She gave me the coordinates.

"Anything else?" she asked.

"No."

"Stay safe."

CHAPTER 26
BELLINGHAM, WASHINGTON
THE YEAR 2015

I drove to Marine Park at the edge of Fairhaven. Marine Park was located right on Bellingham's bay, and I liked to sit in my car and watch the water. The sea always relaxed me, and I thought it was a peaceful and secluded place to remote view.

Pushing back my seat, I put the clipboard and pencil in my lap and felt the Herkimer that was suspended from my neck. I looked at the coordinates on the paper in front of me, studying the information until I had it memorized. I took a deep breath and began to visualize what I was going to do.

Ann, it's just like when you try to remember where you might have left your car keys. It's that easy, I coached myself.

With a clean sheet on the clipboard in front, I began my TM ritual. I then followed it with the remote viewing.

I could see a four-lane highway dead end into a mountainside cave. Catty-corner was an enormous paved parking lot; it was at least two acres in size. The parking lot was a staging area for building materials. Obviously something was being built inside the cave. There was also a helipad painted on the lot off to one side. At the cave's entrance, there was a huge arched tunnel with massive stone and steel doors. The doors were closed.

Inside was a self-contained government facility, equipped with its own geothermal power generator. There were bunking rooms, food storage, and an indoor greenhouse to grow food. Clearly the facility was intended to remain running 24/7 and was protected from outside harm.

Inside the gigantic cave, there were two digital-media rooms, where the RFID storage-array networks were housed. One storage array was for live data, and the other was a mirror of the original database. The second was an emergency machine, used to restore the original data if something corrupted it. The network arrays were nearly perfect; they were isolated from the main database, and information would flow at the speed of light from the data center to this media room.

I began to look inside the RFID array to find a root directory. After finding it, I saw the subdirectory named *privacy*.

The privacy folder listed a multitude of indexes and folders that stored all the RFID and personal tracking data the government had collected—it was all there. I saw the privacy folder, and then I visualized each record as it was stored on the underlying disk drives, as digital zeros and ones. I had captured the actual storage ability in my mind. Each zero and one represented information stored on the physical location of a magnetic drive that could be turned off, which was represented by a zero, or turned on, which was represented by a one.

I started with the indexes, visualizing compressing the zeros and ones together, until I saw them burst together in a brilliant flash of light. I imagined the light creating its own magnetic field that would jumble up each bit of information with random data. Doing this would not do any physical harm to the disk array, but as far as the actual information went, it would be utterly catastrophic and completely unrecoverable.

This first step destroyed the indexes. I did the same for all the data files in the subdirectories. I followed that action with a cataclysmic destruction of the disk file control block. This was the gem that held the file permissions for the disk drive. I changed all permissions on the disk to read-only, which allowed me to erase the backup nodes before the database automatically tried to restore the corrupt data.

I then moved into the second room, which held the backup storage array. This room, like the one before it, was small and enclosed in concrete, which made it fireproof and also protected it from most disasters.

The data architect would have an exact copy of the RFID data on the storage array in this room. This redundant system gave the government 99.99 percent reliability that the RFID data would always be available. This was an online backup. I destroyed it just as I had the primary data system.

This left one last place to go—the Canadian National Archives. They would have the tape copies there for offsite storage of all digital records for Canada.

I visualized the directories saved on tape and, with a flash in my mind, jumbled all the data on the tapes.

Coming out of the remote view, I immediately made the connection between the data bursting in flashes of magnetic light to watching the Fourth of July fireworks as a kid. I remembered all of us with our ooohs and ahhhs each time they burst.

This was my own Canadian Independence Day. I hoped it worked.

CHAPTER 27
BELLINGHAM, WASHINGTON
THE YEAR 2015

I awoke in a daze. It was Monday morning.

"Sinéad, give me the CNN news."

"Yesterday, President Obama gave a speech at the University of Washington about a new energy bill that he will present to Congress to greatly reduce our reliance on foreign oil…"

Didn't he say that in 2011? I thought, blinking myself awake.

"…He also agreed to temporarily increase the quota for—"

"Stop. Sinéad, give me the news for Canada."

"The new prime minister of Canada has announced that he will back a Family Care Plan to bring Canadians back to their liberal ideals. There is some breaking news also from British Columbia, but sources have yet to confirm it—"

"Stop. Sinéad, tell me everything about the breaking news."

"The driver's licensing offices have all closed their doors in B.C., giving the cause as a power disruption, but it has affected all driver's licensing offices across the Province. Also, the Passport Canada offices closed their doors today, giving a power outage as the cause—"

"Stop."

I bolted upright in my bed. Pulling the covers aside, I swung my legs over the edge of the bed, stepping down onto the floor.

"Woohoo!" I screamed at the top of my lungs.

Lulu charged in the bedroom, barking.

"Woohoo, woohoo, woohoo!" I shouted. "Baby, you would have been proud of me," I said aloud to Armond.

Lulu barked some more.

"That's a gift for you, Shorty," I said aloud to the Canadian candidate I'd tested.

I was filled with unbridled elation. It was a victory for GOG, Shorty, and all Canadian citizens.

Dashing into the kitchen, I grabbed some beef from the freezer, defrosted it in the microwave, and cooked it up for Lulu as a special treat. I made myself buttermilk waffles. We sat on the floor and had a party to celebrate the victory, basking in the joy of not only what I had done, but also what I was now capable of. Maybe I wasn't just a weapon to the U.S. Government. Maybe I was a weapon for the good of mankind, to help bring personal liberty back. Maybe I could be a force for good.

"Ann, it's eight forty-five," Sinéad warned me.

"Oh man—I gotta get ready for work," I exclaimed, shooting up from the floor.

At ten was an all-hands meeting with Bennett and department heads. After quickly showering, I headed to my closet to throw some clothes on.

Delight enveloped me on my drive to work as I thought about my accomplishment.

By nine thirty, I was at my desk—only a half hour late. Bennett agreed to my working flextime, so the time I arrived didn't really matter. When I came down the 1910's stairs, I noticed that Paul was not at his desk, nor was Edwin. Edwin had never been late (that I knew of) in the three years he'd worked at AlterHydro, so that was odd.

After checking my voicemail and email, I grabbed a pen and paper and headed up to the meeting. Lulu stayed in her bed. As I came in the conference-room door, both Edwin and Paul followed me in, having just arrived.

Remembering our closeness at my house, I couldn't help but be happy. That combined with my remote-viewing achievement…it was almost hard for me to think straight. I sat down at the conference table, and Paul sat down next to me. I said hello to him, trying my best to keep our co-worker boundary.

In the conference room stood an oblong table surrounded by ten chairs. The head of the table was open, and there was a laptop set up for a presentation. I said hello to all the department heads. Raymond sat on the other side of me, and I chitchatted with him.

Bennett and his brother entered the room together. Bennett greeted everyone and gave me a nod and a smile.

He definitely has a thing for me.

I wanted to laugh out loud and say, "Not a chance," but I just smiled back at him. His brother didn't say a thing, except to nod at Paul and greet the person next to him.

"Thanks everyone for being here on time," Bennett started.

As I tuned in to listen, Paul intimately pressed his knee to mine under the table. I took my booted foot and slowly smashed it against his shoe as hard as I could, intending to send him a message to knock it off at work. From the corner of my eye, I saw him wince and then smile. He got the message.

Even though I had the live wire next to me, I was able to focus on Bennett's presentation, answering questions that Bennett had about the technical manual and Brock's confrontational questions about the manual's completion schedule.

My mind kept drifting back to the Canadian RFID destruction. It still blew my mind that I could remote view, changing reality. I was pondering this when Bennett asked a question. I realized everyone was looking at me.

"What?" I asked, turning my head toward my boss.

"You must not have heard me, Ann."

"I'm sorry, Bennett. I was working through something in the manual in my head."

Brock snickered.

Jerk.

"I asked whether the specs for the testing were back from China."

"Oh, yes, I just got them in email late last week. After I correct the English, it'll be ready for Edwin."

"When will that be?"

"I can move that project up and have it ready for him by tomorrow, if that'll work."

"Great," Bennett responded with a smile.

I nodded.

The meeting continued, and we finished up at eleven thirty, when Bennett said that he was treating us to pizza at La Fiamma.

Mmm. I love their pizza with smoked salmon and roasted garlic.

Bennett advised everyone to meet there at noon.

CHAPTER 28
BELLINGHAM, WASHINGTON
THE YEAR 2015

The doorbell rang at exactly seven p.m.

I opened the door, and immediately a hand holding a bouquet of wildflowers slid through.

"I'm sorry for…I'm sorry for the public affection," Paul grinned, a little sheepishly.

I had to laugh. "You're forgiven," I responded.

He gave me a big smile.

"You're easy," he gushed, happy about my forgiveness.

"I wasn't really mad. I just wanted to let you know that when we're at work, I need to focus on work, not you."

"My foot *still* hurts," he said, feigning a limp.

I smacked him playfully on the shoulder.

"I gotta tell you, Paul, I really like it that you're on time."

"Thank you. Did you love that pizza today, or what?" he asked, stepping inside.

"Yes. I'm salivating right now, thinking of it."

"So, what are we eating tonight?" Paul asked.

"Pizza."

"Pizza?" he asked.

I tried not to laugh at his disappointed expression. "Just kidding…I was thinking about cooking up some steaks and asparagus on the grill, and I was going to make some sea scallops for appetizers. I thought we'd have a tossed salad with the steaks. How does that sound?"

"Now *I'm* salivating," he responded cheerfully. "What can I help you with?"

"Are you a guy who grills?"

"I was *made* to grill."

I laughed. I gave him the marinated steaks, tongs, and asparagus, and sent him to the back patio.

"Sinéad, play a U2 mix."

"Isn't Sinéad gonna be jealous you're not playing her music?" he asked, calling over his shoulder.

I chuckled. *I never thought of that.*

Paul finished grilling, and I had the scallops and salad ready. We sat at the kitchen island to eat.

"You must have heard about the chaos at the Canadian driver's licensing offices," Paul said.

"I did. When I picked up the dinner ingredients at the Co-Op, my friend was telling me all about it. You must be thrilled about the news," I said, prodding.

"I am. For such a thing to happen is a…gift," he stated sincerely.

A gift.

"Hmmm. I think you're right."

Paul turned to me and looked directly into my eyes. "They want to meet you in Portland tomorrow morning at one in the afternoon," he blurted out.

I just looked back at him.

Does he mean…

My heart started to race. "Who wants to meet me?"

"The parents."

"What? Who?" I asked, panicked that Paul wasn't who I thought he was.

Previously, I had always been contacted directly by GOG. They would usually leave a note for me in my house with a call-in number, or leave me a note in some other way.

Is Paul government?

"I know they don't usually contact you like this. But this is an unusual event, as you know. Ann…I've known for a very long time."

"Known what?"

"I saw you three years ago at the Gaslight Brasserie. I know about the meeting."

I could feel the heavy beating of my heart and wondered if Paul could hear it.

"Who are you?" I said, moving slightly away from him.

"It was my job that day—outer electronic security. I was parked outside the back of the restaurant with electronic equipment, jamming any possible peekers. I'm part of the organization, Ann."

"Tulips," I said, challenging him with the code word, looking directly at him.

I needed to know that he was really GOG.

"Skagit," he immediately replied, confirming the code word. "Now are you satisfied?" he asked, moving closer.

"I am," I said, embarrassed that I had doubted him. "Why didn't you tell me before?" I asked quietly.

"You already know the answer to that," he said.

In the organization, we were not supposed to voluntarily share our membership status with anyone, no matter how close they were. The only real way to know other members was to work on jobs together. That was the only way it was supposed to happen. Such cautions enhanced the likelihood that the organization would remain secret from the government, and it made penetration of GOG very difficult for outsiders.

"So you've known for three years?" I asked, peering into his eyes.

"Yes."

"That's why you were at the Pan Pacific that weekend."

"Yes. I had a very slight feeling that you could be part of the organization. I mean, what's the chance that we would both be a few blocks from the Gaslight Brasserie the day of the job? When we passed the restaurant during our walk, you looked at it as we passed, and I had a strong suspicion that you were there for the same reason I was."

I realized suddenly what this meant. No longer did I have to keep so many things about my life a secret. I could be who I was without being so guarded. Well…at least while I was in my house with Paul. *What a relief.* I could finally trust another person.

"Would you like me to go with you to Portland? I'm assuming you're going to take a personal day. I can do the same," he eagerly asked.

"That would be wonderful," I said with a smile.

"Your flight is already booked to Portland. You're leaving on the nine ten a.m. flight from Bellingham, Alaska Air. Let me see if I can grab a seat on that flight."

"What time does the flight land in Oregon?"

"Eleven fifty. It connects in Seattle."

"Sinéad, does the nine ten a.m. flight departing from Bellingham to Portland have one more seat?"

"Yes. There are nine seats open on the Bellingham flight, and three open seats on the Seattle-to-Portland flight."

"Let me book it," Paul interrupted as he pulled out his iPhone, looked up the flight, and booked the ticket as I watched his face. He was all business.

"All done," he announced with a smile.

"Do you think anyone will suspect anything, with both of us gone on the same day?"

"If you're taking a personal day, I'll call in sick. That way no one will suspect anything."

"That's a good plan. You'd better start coughing."

"I'll call in the morning—I'll have worked up a sore throat by then. If I stay here till three a.m., I won't need to work up a frog in my throat—I'll have one from lack of sleep," he joked, giving me a wink.

As I watched his mouth move in that delicious way, with his eyes sparkling playfully, I felt my body respond.

"What?" he asked with a curious expression.

"You're really something," I said, smiling.

He moved closer to me, until he was a couple of inches from my face. "You're pretty terrific yourself," he quietly responded. He looked into my eyes and then planted a juicy, lingering kiss on my lips.

Chemistry, I thought as I enjoyed his mouth on mine, with the taste of lemonade—sweet and tart like that first kiss—enduring.

He backed away slowly, opening his eyes to look at me again. "Wow. If that's any indication of what's to come, then…" he said, smiling wide.

"What?" I asked, returning his smile.

"Oh…nothing," he said, adjusting himself in his seat. "There is something I want to know."

"What?"

"I want to know how you did it," he said, looking at me intensely.

"Did what?"

"You know what."

"Can't I have *any* secrets?" I teased.

"You can, just not that one. I am *dying* to know how you did the RFID hack. I want details."

I told him all about my remote-viewing success.

"You know the offices in Canada have been closed all day?"

"I know, isn't it great? If they're closed down, they can't issue any more RFID licenses."

"They haven't released anything to the press yet, so no one knows what's happened. Hopefully tomorrow, in Portland, we'll learn something from the inside about what you actually achieved."

"I can't wait to find out," I said, giddy. "Hey, you wanna take Lulu for a walk? It's so pretty outside, and sunset will be soon."

"Sure. Just give me a minute to finish this steak."

CHAPTER 29
BELLINGHAM, WASHINGTON
THE YEAR 2015

Paul and I agreed to meet on the plane at the Bellingham terminal to avoid any suspicion that we were flying together. I dropped Lulu off at Aunt Saundra's for the day. She and I had a very early breakfast together, visiting.

While driving to the airport, I decided to call Bob. I had a particular question for him.

"Hello?"

"Well aren't I a lucky girl to get you to answer your phone?" I teased.

"I think the luck is mine," Bob replied, sweet-talking me.

"I have a question for you."

"Go ahead."

"The location. Why were they a target?"

"The building was built with a full basement—unusual for that part of Shanghai, since it was prone to typhoon floods. We'd always watched it because of activity there."

"But why is it a target *now*?"

"You should know the answer to that, Ann."

"You mean that what I originally saw was again taking place the day of my dream?" I said, remembering that the first time I remote viewed into the Bund Hotel, there was a meeting in the basement.

Because of Yang Li's loss of his soulmate, he built the basement so that the Chinese underground could fight against the establishment.

"Presumably so. I don't know for sure, but I'm guessing it's very likely."

"I understand. Thank you, Bob."

"Ann?"

"Yeah?"

"Now I have something to ask you."

"What is it?" I asked, curious.

"Have you been traveling recently, eh?" he asked with a Canadian interjection.

"You know, it's very rainy there," I replied, unwilling to answer his question on an unsecured phone.

"It certainly is," he responded forcefully.

"Was there anything else?" I asked, hoping that he wouldn't press me.

"Be careful. Ask yourself why I would be asking the question in the first place."

"Okay, Bob."

"Stay dry, Ann."

"Bye."

Hanging up, I was shaken by his question. The only way Bob could know about my connection to the Canadian RFID hack was if the other agency was viewing it.

"Well, there's nothing I can do about it now," I said out loud, trying to reassure myself.

I arrived at Bellingham airport at eight a.m., parked, and was in the terminal check-in line by eight ten. That was a benefit to the tiny airport; I only had to show up an hour before the flight. As I was waiting in line, my phone rang.

"Hello?"

"Ann, it's Paul."

"Hey there," I said cheerfully.

"I'm not going to be able to make it. I've been at the company since five this morning. We had a server crash. I thought I'd be able to get it back up in time, but it's more complicated than that."

"That's okay. I know where I'm going. I'll see you when I get back."

"Okay, bye," he said, sounding stressed and rushed.

"Bye."

I was looking forward to his company and being able to meet with GOG together. I stepped forward to check-in for the flight. I had about a half hour before my flight would board, so I decided to call Elinor at college.

"Hello?"

"Hey, it's Mom," I said, exuberant that I had caught her instead of voicemail.

"Hi, Mom."

"I had a few minutes and thought I'd check in and see how you and your sweetie are."

"It's so good to hear your voice, Mom. We are both great—terrific, actually."

"Oh, I'm so glad, Elinor."

We talked for about fifteen minutes. Elinor caught me up on school details and what she and Eliott had been up to. He hadn't popped the question yet, but Elinor was sure he was ring shopping.

"Mom, I love you and miss you."

"I love you, too," I said. "Tell Eliott 'hi' for me and give him a hug. You two take care of each other," I said.

"Okay. Bye."

"Bye."

I loved my little girl. Maybe she wasn't little anymore, but she would always be my sweet little girl.

They called for the flight to board, and I stepped into the line. It was a short flight to Seattle, only twenty-five minutes—a prop plane for this route. I never really knew whether I'd get a bumpy ride on this hop or not, but today the skies looked clear. As we took to the air, I looked out the window and saw the San Juan Islands below. Seeing them from the air always made me tenderly remember sailing the islands with Armond and Elinor in those perfect days. About ten minutes into the flight, we entered a Seattle-area storm, and the turbulence began. I always noticed how other passengers who didn't fly this route regularly would look a little green at this point. My own gut was rock solid, whether I was in heavy turbulence flying or in rough ocean swells below. This flight seemed like a roller-coaster ride, unexpected and fun.

When we landed at Seattle airport, some passengers were definitely peaked. After letting those who seemed in a hurry go in front of me, I exited onto the tarmac and walked up the stairs to the terminal. I looked for the boarding gate; it wasn't far from my arrival gate, and I only had twenty minutes to wait. I did some people watching, which was always fun. Seattle was such an eclectic city, filled with all sorts of colorful people.

We finally started to board the jet for Portland, and it looked like a completely full flight. Sinéad had moved me into the window seat of the emergency exit. It was the perfect place to sit because it had the most legroom, and there were no seats in front to recline and take up all my space. I didn't care if it was a full flight, as long as I had my window seat and some legroom.

The takeoff was a little rough, due to the storm that had moved in. The sky was dark. We had some turbulence during the flight, but it wasn't horrible. Being in a Boeing 717 commuter jet was much better than being in a prop plane.

"So what are you doing in Portland?" the blond woman next to me asked.

"Just going down for a day trip," I replied, giving no information.

"I'm going down for a meeting…" she offered, trying to generate conversation.

"And who do you work for?" I asked, obliging.

"Microsoft. I direct sales for a new product line," she replied, boasting.

She's doing well at Microsoft, I thought, looking at her.

Blondie was about my age and height, but she looked a little anorexic. She quite obviously had some plastic surgery help with her bosom, as I could see the outline of her ribs below her size D. She wore enormous diamonds in her engagement and wedding rings, a diamond bracelet, and though I couldn't tell for certain, I was sure her clothes came from an expensive designer.

She continued, "I do well there, but I have a two-year-old daughter, and I wish I didn't have to travel so much, so I could spend more time with her. Right now, I think she spends more time with the nanny than with me."

"Oh, that's sad," I said sincerely, looking at her.

"I know. It took four series of in-vitro fertilization before it took, and now that I have her, it's just *so much work*! I don't know what I'd do without the nanny," she said, perplexed.

For twenty minutes, Blondie continued exposing her personal information, telling me how her husband wasn't that interested in sex since she'd had their child and how difficult her team at Microsoft was to deal with. I tuned out, being ill-equipped to lend compassion to this woman who was my antithesis. I realized that we hadn't even exchanged names. It was only a fifty-minute flight, but she was quickly exhausting me.

Forty minutes into the flight, we started bouncing all over the sky. Other passengers near me were visibly disturbed, as was Blondie; I could tell from her white knuckles as she gripped our joint armrest. It was the worst turbulence I had ever been in. I knew it was pretty bad by the silence from the pilot and copilot. I rode the swells. Blondie abruptly stopped talking, which I was grateful for.

Our plane was not only dropping altitude from time to time, but it was listing and pitching, seemingly uncontrollably. I watched out the window, and as I did so, our jet took a direct hit from lightning—right on the wing—close to my window. It blinded me and lighted up the inside of the plane. I immediately felt energy move through the wing and into the cabin; I had never felt anything like that before. At that same moment, thunder overcame every other sound, including the jet engines; I could feel the deep sound resonate in my chest. My seatmate grabbed my arm and squeezed, cutting her faux nails into my flesh. Immediately after the lightening hit, the pitching became more radical. Passengers panicked, huddling close to one another out of fear. My seatmate was pushing her shoulder against mine, and she held on to my arm for dear life. Her foot was pushed up on the seat in front of her, trying to stabilize her skinny frame from the lurching.

Not long after the strike, the pilot came over the speaker, saying, "Yes, folks, we were just hit by lightning, but we've checked out all our systems, and everything is operational. We are continuing into Portland. Since we're still in turbulence, stay seated."

"Turbulence?" one passenger behind us shouted incredulously.

We were still jumping all over the sky, and I thought my blond companion was going to barf all over me.

As our jet was on approach for Portland airport, we were still lurching up and down. Just before the wheels touched down, the jet suddenly pitched, starting to turn sideways, one wing up and one wing down, and we began to twist, as though we would cartwheel sideways.

The cabin filled with the terror of people screaming, praying, and crying. Luggage large and small tumbled from the overhead bins and was thrown all over the cabin. I dodged someone's purse and turned to look out my window. The wing was about to hit the tarmac.

I was surprised that I felt no fear.

Instead, I felt an inexplicable sense of peace. I knew that we would not live through the crash, and in a nanosecond I remembered flashes from my life with Armond, Elinor, Dad, Aunt Saundra, and others. Falling in love in São Paulo…Elinor's birth…sailing the San Juans in the *Woohoo*…kayaking with Orcas…eating at the Red Sea restaurant with Armond and my friends…swing dancing at Glen Echo Park…skiing….

Then I remembered Armond's last words. "The Herkimer," he'd said. "Believe…." And I reached up to feel the crystal hanging from the chain around my neck.

ABOUT THE AUTHOR

The Prophecies series you're reading, or deciding whether you should read, was born just after the author survived a near crash in a passenger jet. Thankfully, she lived to write this trilogy.

Before Linda Hawley became a full-time author, she supported herself as a freelance writer. Her experiences working on diverse projects requiring significant research stretched and refined her composition skills. It also inspired her to become a novelist.

You may be surprised to learn that most of the technologies, conditions, and places in her trilogy exist. It's the characters and their actions that are pure fiction. Writing The Prophecies as accurate faction (a literary work that is a mix of fact and fiction) requires significant in-depth research, but the author was aided by her many years in the U.S. intelligence community. Her government service certainly aided the believability of this dystopian trilogy.

Linda Hawley is hard at work on another dystopian trilogy, called The ReSociety. You can follow her progress at LindaHawley.com.

THE PROPHECIES TRILOGY

To view insider's tidbits of The Prophecies, read an interview with the author, and ask questions about the series, visit:
LindaHawley.com

Follow the author on Twitter: *Twitter.com/LindaHawley*

Follow the author on Facebook: *Facebook.com/TheProphecies Series*

The author enjoys receiving email from readers at:
Linda@LindaHawley.com

If you've enjoyed this novel, please take a minute and review it at the retail store where it was purchased.

Made in the USA
Charleston, SC
04 October 2012